THROUGH THE LOOKING GLASS

Lewis Carroll

COLLINS
CLASSICS

Harper Press
An imprint of HarperCollins*Publishers*
77–85 Fulham Palace Road
Hammersmith
London W6 8JB

This edition published 2010

A catalogue record for this book is available from the British Library

ISBN-13: 978-0-00-735093-3

Printed and bound in Great Britain by Clays Ltd, St Ives plc

Mixed Sources
Product group from well-managed
forests and other controlled sources
www.fsc.org Cert no. SW-COC-001806
© 1996 Forest Stewardship Council

FSC is a non-profit international organisation established to promote the
responsible management of the world's forests. Products carrying the FSC
label are independently certified to assure consumers that they come
from forests that are managed to meet the social, economic and
ecological needs of present and future generations.

Find out more about HarperCollins and the environment at
www.harpercollins.co.uk/green

Life & Times section © Gerard Cheshire
Classic Literature: Words and Phrases adapted from
Collins English Dictionary
Typesetting in Kalix by Palimpsest Book Production Limited,
Grangemouth, Stirlingshire

History of Collins

In 1819, Millworker William Collins from Glasgow, Scotland, set up a company for printing and publishing pamphlets, sermons, hymn books and prayer books. That company was Collins and was to mark the birth of HarperCollins Publishers as we know it today. The long tradition of Collins dictionary publishing can be traced back to the first dictionary William published in 1824, *Greek and English Lexicon*. Indeed, from 1840 onwards, he began to produce illustrated dictionaries and even obtained a licence to print and publish the Bible.

Soon after, William published the first Collins novel, *Ready Reckoner*, however it was the time of the Long Depression, where harvests were poor, prices were high, potato crops had failed and violence was erupting in Europe. As a result, many factories across the country were forced to close down and William chose to retire in 1846, partly due to the hardships he was facing.

Aged 30, William's son, William II took over the business. A keen humanitarian with a warm heart and a generous spirit, William II was truly 'Victorian' in his outlook. He introduced new, up-to-date steam presses and published affordable editions of Shakespeare's works and *Pilgrim's Progress*, making them available to the masses for the first time. A new demand for educational books meant that success came with the publication of travel books, scientific books, encyclopaedias and dictionaries. This demand to be educated led to the later publication of atlases and Collins also held the monopoly on scripture writing at the time.

In the 1860s Collins began to expand and diversify and the idea of 'books for the millions' was developed. Affordable editions of classical literature were published and in 1903 Collins introduced 10 titles in their Collins Handy Illustrated Pocket Novels. These proved so popular that a few years later this had increased to an output of 50 volumes, selling nearly half a million in their year of publication. In the same year, The Everyman's Library was also instituted, with the idea of publishing an affordable library of the most important classical works, biographies, religious and philosophical treatments, plays, poems, travel and adventure. This series eclipsed all competition at the time and the introduction of paperback books in the 1950s helped to open that market and marked a high point in the industry.

HarperCollins is and has always been a champion of the classics and the current Collins Classics series follows in this tradition – publishing classical literature that is affordable and available to all. Beautifully packaged, highly collectible and intended to be reread and enjoyed at every opportunity.

Life & Times

About the Author

The author of Lewis Carroll's *Alice's Adventures in Wonderland* and *Through The Looking Glass* was in fact a Charles Ludwidge Dodgson (1832–98). He published under the pseudonym Lewis Carroll because he wished to maintain anonymity and so remain relatively immune to any criticism of his poetry and prose. He actually came up with his pen name by translating his first two names into Latin 'Carolus Lodovicus' and then Anglicizing them to 'Lewis Carroll', a perfect example of his love for the playfulness of language.

Charles Dodgson's place of birth was a parsonage in the county of Cheshire, England, as his father was an Anglican parson. The family moved to the county of Yorkshire when he was eleven, by which time Queen Victoria had been on the throne for four years.

He and his siblings were home tutored which had an inevitable effect on their ability to socialize. All of the children also suffered from speech stammering. As a result, this self-consciousness was something that pervaded and continued to affect Charles for the rest of his life.

For two years Dodgson attended a school in Richmond, Yorkshire, and then he was sent to Rugby School at the age of fourteen. Like his father, he showed great promise as a mathematician and went on to academic success at Oxford University, even winning a lectureship, which kept him fiscally well off for many years.

Like his father, he decided to enter the church and became an Anglican deacon at Christ Church, Oxford, although his relationship with Christianity was one with which he wrestled. He was, at heart, a liberal thinker, as his literary work would eventually betray.

As well as his stammer, which he referred to as his 'hesitation', he was also deaf in one ear and had a weak chest, resulting from childhood ailments. It may well have been these psychological and physical flaws that translated into his drive to succeed as a writer and him becoming a prominent member of society.

Having always written short stories and drawn illustrations, Dodgson began publishing his own magazine in 1855 as a means of creative expression. It was titled the *Mischmasch* (German for 'mishmash') as the magazine was a mishmash of ideas designed for the amusement of his family. Then, in 1856, he had the opportunity to officially publish some work in *The Train: A First-Class Magazine*, which was a short lived monthly magazine and prompted him to invent his pseudonym Lewis Carroll.

It was at this time that Dodgson became acquainted with a new colleague, Henry Liddell, and his young family. It's likely that he felt less intimidated by children, and so was probably less self conscious about his stammer. Dodgson grew very fond of Liddell's son and three daughters and they proved to be the perfect audience for his imaginative stories. It was in this way that he was encouraged to write *Alice's Adventures in Wonderland*. The story goes that he orated the first version to Liddell's three daughters, Lorina, Alice and Edith, whilst on a boat trip and it was Alice Liddell who urged him to commit the adventures to paper. It took him three years to complete the manuscript to his satisfaction and to finally have the book published in 1865. The book quickly caught the collective imagination of Victorian society and became something of a publishing sensation. In fact, it has never been out of print and has been translated into almost every language, such is its universal popularity.

In 1871 Dodgson published a new book about Alice, titled *Through the Looking Glass and What Alice Found There*. Apparently his inspiration was another conversation with Alice Liddell, where they discussed what it might be like to enter the reflected world in a mirror. Although a sequel to *Alice's Adventures in Wonderland*, there are no references to the events of the first book, but the themes, ideas and characters do seem to echo and mirror those of *Alice's Adventures in Wonderland*. This second book was every bit as successful as the first.

The Victorian Era

There was a paradox about the Victorian era during which Dodgson lived. On the one hand it was conservative and formalized, but on the other it was progressive and dynamic. In 1859 Charles Darwin had published *On the Origin of Species*, in which he had revealed his theory of biological evolution by natural selection. It famously caused a great deal of scientific and theological argument, but it also had the effect of allowing people to think more laterally or outside of the box, because it showed that preconceived ideas may no longer be appropriate or correct.

Dodgson was already a creative mind and it was in this revolutionary environment that he allowed his imagination to ferment the fantastical ideas that would evolve into *Alice's Adventures in Wonderland*. His fertile imaginings were honed by using the Liddell children as his sounding board, so that he developed an instinct for writing prose that appealed to children and adults alike.

His two books about Alice are now described as literary nonsense as he was the first author to allow himself the creative license to go wherever his mind took him. As a result he produced stories that enter absurd worlds with anthropomorphic animals and other strange characters with exaggerated personality traits. All of the time though, Dodgson uses the scenarios to tackle problems relating to logic, reason and philosophical conundrums, so that there is far more to the books than there would immediately seem.

Queen Victoria herself was a fan of Dodgson's work, demonstrating that she and many other Victorians were open to the idea of allowing a little nonsense into their lives. It probably came as a welcome counter balance to the weight of austerity that typified the age in other respects.

Dodgson's work also set a benchmark for new writers. Literary nonsense became a genre in its own right and many subsequent authors have drawn inspiration from Dodgson's ability to delve into his subconscious, almost as if he were taking psychedelic drugs to conjure a dream-like place, that he called Wonderland. In effect, Dodgson realised that literature is a true art form, just like painting or sculpture, in that so-called rules are there only to be tested and reset in the creative process.

Incidentally it seems likely that Dodgson had indeed tried hallucinogenic drugs. Opium smoking dens existed in Victorian London as it was long before the drug was made illegal. In addition to this, it was known that *Psilocybin* mushrooms could be consumed to induce mind bending effects. In the book a shrunken Alice meets a caterpillar, smoking a hookah pipe and reclining on a mushroom. Alice consumes morsels of mushroom that make her first shrink even smaller and then grow back to her normal size. Surely drugs had something to do with such ideas.

Themes of the Book

It is perhaps inevitable that people have read between the lines a great deal with *Alice's Adventures in Wonderland* and *Through The Looking Glass*. That is to say, they have searched for a hidden meaning, agenda or allegory that Dodgson wished to express through his work. It seems more likely though that it is what it is – literary nonsense. The books are an exploration of imagined possibilities.

Dodgson doesn't seem to have harboured any desire to pass comment on Victorian society. Although it is known that many of his literary characters were based on the personalities of his friends, it seems that this was merely an aid to character creation and development rather than any intention to parody them in any way. He was a humanist at heart, so he used his friends because he enjoyed and celebrated their idiosyncrasies and foibles.

It was this encapsulation of the human condition that seems to have made his work so popular, because the characters are in fact familiar stereotypes, so that readers can recognise traits in themselves and in the people they know. What is more, they are ubiquitous traits, so that they exist in people the world over. For example; Alice is the attractively inquisitive and naive girl, the white rabbit is the neurotic clerk, the caterpillar is the laid back artist, and so on.

THROUGH THE
LOOKING GLASS

CONTENTS

Child of the pure unclouded brow
And dreaming eyes of wonder!
Though time be fleet, and I and thou
Are half a life asunder,
Thy loving smile will surely hail
The love-gift of a fairy-tale.

I have not seen thy sunny face,
Nor heard thy silver laughter;
No thought of me shall find a place
In thy young life's hereafter –
Enough that now thou wilt not fail
To listen to my fairy-tale.

A tale begun in other days,
When summer suns were glowing –
A simple chime, that served to time
The rhythm of our rowing –
Whose echoes live in memory yet,
Though envious years would say 'forget.'

Come, hearken then, ere voice of dread,
With bitter tidings laden,
Shall summon to unwelcome bed
A melancholy maiden!
We are but older children, dear,
Who fret to find our bedtime near.

Without, the frost, the blinding snow,
The storm-wind's moody madness –
Within, the firelight's ruddy glow
And childhood's nest of gladness.

The magic words shall hold thee fast:
Thou shalt not heed the raving blast.

And though the shadow of a sigh
May tremble through the story,
For 'happy summer days' gone by,
And vanish'd summer glory –
It shall not touch with breath of bale
The pleasance of our fairy-tale.

AUTHOR'S NOTE

As the chess-problem, given on the next page, has puzzled some of my readers, it may be well to explain that it is correctly worked out, so far as the *moves* are concerned. The *alternation* of Red and White is perhaps not so strictly observed as it might be, and the 'castling' of the three Queens is merely a way of saying that they entered the palace: but the 'check' of the White King at move 6, the capture of the Red Knight at move 7, and the final 'checkmate' of the Red King, will be found, by any one who will take the trouble to set the pieces and play the moves as directed, to be strictly in accordance with the laws of the game.

The new words, in the poem 'Jabberwocky' (see page 175), have given rise to some differences of opinion as to their pronunciation: so it may be well to give instructions on *that* point also. Pronounce 'slithy' as if it were the two words, 'sly, the': make the 'g' *hard* in 'gyre' and 'gimble': and pronounce 'rath' to rhyme with 'bath.'

Christmas, 1896

Dramatis Personae
(As arranged before commencement of game)

WHITE		RED	
PIECES	PAWNS	PAWNS	PIECES
Tweedledee	Daisy	Daisy	Humpty Dumpty
Unicorn	Haigha	Messenger	Carpenter
Sheep	Oyster	Oyster	Walrus
W. Queen	'Lily'	Tiger-lily	R. Queen
W. King	Fawn	Rose	R. King
Aged man	Oyster	Oyster	Crow
W. Knight	Hatta	Frog	R. Knight
Tweedledum	Daisy	Daisy	Lion

RED

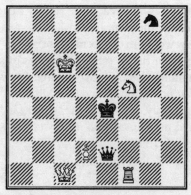

WHITE

White Pawn (Alice) to play, and win in eleven moves

CHAPTER 1

Looking-Glass House

One thing was certain, that the *white* kitten had had nothing to do with it: it was the black kitten's fault entirely. For the white kitten had been having its face washed by the old cat for the last quarter of an hour (and bearing it pretty well, considering); so you see that it *couldn't* have had any hand in the mischief.

The way Dinah washed her children's faces was this: first she held the poor thing down by its ear with one paw, and then with the other paw she rubbed its face all over, the wrong way, beginning at the nose: and just now, as I said, she was hard at work on the white kitten, which was lying quite still and trying to purr – no doubt feeling that it was all meant for its good.

But the black kitten had been finished with earlier in the afternoon, and so, while Alice was sitting curled up in a corner of the great armchair, half talking to herself and half asleep, the kitten had been having a grand game of romps with the ball of worsted Alice had been trying to wind up, and had been rolling it up and down till it had all come undone again; and there it was, spread over the hearth-rug, all knots and tangles, with the kitten running after its own tail in the middle.

'Oh, you wicked, wicked little thing!' cried Alice, catching up the kitten, and giving it a little kiss to make it understand that it was in disgrace. 'Really, Dinah ought to have taught you better manners! You *ought*, Dinah, you know you ought!' she added, looking reproachfully at the old cat, and speaking in as cross a voice as she could manage – and then she scrambled back into the armchair, taking the kitten and the worsted with her, and began winding up the ball again. But she didn't get on very fast, as she was talking all the time, sometimes to the kitten, and sometimes to herself. Kitty sat very demurely on her knee, pretending to watch the progress of the winding, and now and then putting out one paw and gently touching the ball, as if it would be glad to help if it might.

'Do you know what tomorrow is, Kitty?' Alice began. 'You'd have guessed if you'd been up in the window with me – only Dinah, was making you tidy, so you couldn't. I was watching the boys getting in sticks for the bonfire – and it wants plenty of sticks, Kitty!

Only it got so cold, and it snowed so, they had to leave off. Never mind, Kitty, we'll go and see the bonfire tomorrow.' Here Alice wound two or three turns of the worsted round the kitten's neck, just to see how it would look: this led to a scramble, in which the ball rolled down upon the floor, and yards and yards of it got unwound again.

'Do you know, I was so angry, Kitty,' Alice went on, as soon as they were comfortably settled again, 'when I saw all the mischief you had been doing, I was very nearly opening the window, and putting you out into the snow! And you'd have deserved it, you little mischievous darling! What have you got to say for your-self? Now don't interrupt me!' she went on, holding up one finger. 'I'm going to tell you all your faults. Number one: you squeaked twice while Dinah was washing your face this morning. Now you can't deny it, Kitty, I heard you! What's that you say?' (pretending that the kitten was speaking.) 'Her paw went into your eye? Well, that's *your* fault, for keeping your eyes open – if you'd shut them tight up, it wouldn't have happened. Now don't make any more excuses, but listen! Number two: you pulled Snowdrop away by the tail just as I had put down the saucer of milk before her! What, you were thirsty, were you? How do you know she wasn't thirsty too? Now for number three: you unwound every bit of the worsted while I wasn't looking!

'That's three faults, Kitty, and you've not been punished for any of them yet. You know I'm saving up all your punishments for Wednesday week – Suppose they had saved up all *my* punishments!' she went on, talking more to herself than the kitten. 'What *would* they do at the end of a year? I should be sent to prison, I suppose, when the day came. Or – let me see – suppose each punishment was to be going without a dinner: then, when the miserable day came, I should have to go without fifty dinners at once! Well, I shouldn't mind *that* much! I'd far rather go without them than eat them!

'Do you hear the snow against the window panes, Kitty? How nice and soft it sounds! Just as if some one was kissing the window all over outside. I wonder if the snow *loves* the trees and fields, that it kisses them so gently? And then it covers them up snug, you know, with a white quilt; and perhaps it says "Go to sleep, darlings, till the summer comes again." And when they wake up in the summer, Kitty, they dress themselves all in green, and dance about – whenever the wind blows – oh, that's very pretty!' cried Alice, dropping the ball of worsted to clap her hands. 'And I do so *wish* it was true! I'm sure the woods look sleepy in the autumn, when the leaves are getting brown.

'Kitty, can you play chess? Now, don't smile, my dear, I'm asking it seriously. Because, when we were playing just now, you watched just as if you understood it: and when I said "Check!" you purred! Well, it *was* a nice check, Kitty, and really I might have won, if it hadn't been for that nasty Knight, that came wriggling down

among my pieces. Kitty, dear, let's pretend –' And here I wish I could tell you half the things Alice used to say, beginning with her favourite phrase, 'Let's pretend.' She had had quite a long argument with her sister only the day before – all because Alice had begun with 'Let's pretend we're kings and queens;' and her sister, who liked being very exact, had argued that they couldn't, because there were only two of them, and Alice had been reduced at last to say, 'Well, *you* can be one of them then, and *I'll* be all the rest.' And once she had really frightened her old nurse by shouting suddenly in her ear, 'Nurse! Do let's pretend that I'm a hungry hyena, and you're a bone!'

But this is taking us away from Alice's speech to the kitten. 'Let's pretend that you're the Red Queen, Kitty! Do you know, I think, if you sat up and folded your arms, you'd look exactly like her. Now do try, there's a dear!' And Alice got the Red Queen off the table, and set it up before the kitten as a model for it to imitate: however, the thing didn't succeed, principally, Alice said, because the kitten wouldn't fold its arms properly. So, to punish it, she held it up to the Looking-Glass, that it might see how sulky it was ' – and if you're not good directly,' she added, 'I'll put you through into Looking-Glass House. How would you like *that*?

'Now, if you'll only attend, Kitty, and not talk so much, I'll tell you all my ideas about Looking-Glass House. First, there's the room you can see through the glass – that's just the same as our drawing-room, only the things go the other way. I can see all of it when I get upon a chair – all but the bit just behind the fire-place. Oh! I do so wish I could see *that* bit! I want so much to know whether they've a fire in the winter: you never *can* tell, you know, unless our fire smokes, and then smoke comes up in that room too – but that may be only pretence, just to make it look as if they had a fire. Well then, the books are something like our books, only the words go the wrong way; I know that, because I've held up one of our books to the glass, and then they hold up one in the other room.

'How would you like to live in Looking-Glass House, Kitty? I wonder if they'd give you milk in there? Perhaps Looking-Glass milk isn't good to drink – But oh, Kitty! now we come to the passage. You can just see a little *peep* of the passage in Looking-Glass House, if you leave the door of our drawing-room wide open: and it's very like our passage as far as you can see, only you know it may be quite different on beyond. Oh, Kitty! how nice it would be if we could only get through into Looking-Glass House! I'm sure it's got, oh! such beautiful things in it! Let's pretend there's a way of getting through into it somehow, Kitty. Let's pretend the glass has got all soft like gauze, so that we can get through. Why, it's turning into a sort of mist now, I declare! It'll be easy enough to get through –' She was up on the chimney-piece while she said this, though she hardly knew how she had got there. And certainly the glass *was* beginning to melt away, just like a bright silvery mist.

In another moment Alice was through the glass, and had jumped lightly down into the Looking-Glass room. The very first thing she did was to look whether there was a fire in the fire-place, and she was quite pleased to find that there was a real one, blazing away as brightly as the one she had left behind. 'So I shall be as warm here as I was in the old room,' thought Alice: 'warmer, in fact, because there'll be no one here to scold me away

from the fire. Oh, what fun it'll be when they see me through the glass in here, and can't get at me!'

Then she began looking about, and noticed that what could be seen from the old room was quite common and uninteresting, but that all the rest was as different as possible. For instance, the pictures on the wall next the fire seemed to be all alive, and the very clock on the chimney-piece (you know you can only see the back of it in the looking-glass) had got the face of a little old man and grinned at her.

'They don't keep this room so tidy as the other,' Alice thought to herself, as she noticed several of the chessmen down in the hearth among the cinders: but in another moment, with a little 'Oh!' of surprise she was down on her hands and knees watching them. The chessmen were walking about two and two!

'Here are the Red King and the Red Queen,' Alice said (in a whisper, for fear of frightening them), 'and there are the White King and the White Queen sitting on the edge of the shovel – and there are two Castles walking arm in arm – I don't think they can hear me,' she went on, as she put her head closer down, 'and I'm nearly sure they can't see me. I feel somehow as if I was getting invisible –'

Here something began squeaking on the table behind Alice, and made her turn her head just in time to see one of the White Pawns roll over and begin kicking: she watched it with great curiosity to see what would happen next.

'It is the voice of my child!' the White Queen cried out, as she rushed past the King, so violently that she knocked him over among the cinders. 'My precious Lily! My imperial kitten!' and she began scrambling wildly up the side of the fender.

'Imperial fiddlestick!' said the King, rubbing his nose, which had been hurt by the fall. He had a right to be a *little* annoyed with the Queen, for he was covered with ashes from head to foot.

Alice was very anxious to be of use, and, as the poor little Lily was nearly screaming herself into a fit, she hastily picked up the Queen and set her on the table by the side of her noisy little daughter.

The Queen gasped, and sat down: the rapid journey through the air had quite taken away her breath, and for a minute or two she could do nothing but hug the little Lily in silence. As soon as she had recovered her

breath a little, she called out to the White King, who was sitting sulkily among the ashes, 'Mind the volcano!'

'What volcano?' said the King, looking up anxiously into the fire as if he thought that was the most likely place to find one.

'Blew – me – up,' panted the Queen, who was still a little out of breath. 'Mind you come up – the regular way – don't get blown up!'

Alice watched the White King as he slowly struggled up from bar to bar, till at last she said, 'Why, you'll be hours and hours getting to the table, at that rate. I'd far better help you, hadn't I?' But the King took no notice of the question: it was quite clear that he could neither hear her nor see her.

So Alice picked him up very gently, and lifted him across more slowly than she had lifted the Queen, that she mightn't take his breath away: but, before she put him on the table, she thought she might as well dust him a little, he was so covered with ashes.

She said afterwards that she had never seen in all her life such a face as the King made, when he found himself held in the air by an invisible hand, and being dusted: he was far too much astonished to cry out, but his eyes and his mouth went on getting larger and larger, and rounder and rounder, till her hand shook so with laughing that she nearly let him drop upon the floor.

'Oh! *please* don't make such faces, my dear!' she cried out, quite forgetting that the King couldn't hear her. 'You make me laugh so that I can hardly hold you! And don't keep your mouth so wide open! All the ashes will get into it – there, now I think you're tidy enough!' she added, as she smoothed his hair, and set him upon the table near the Queen.

The King immediately fell flat on his back, and lay perfectly still: and Alice was a little alarmed at what she had done, and went round the room to see if she could find any water to throw over him. However, she could find nothing but a bottle of ink, and when she got back with

it she found he had recovered, and he and the Queen were talking together in a frightened whisper – so low that Alice could hardly hear what they said.

The King was saying, 'I assure you, my dear, I turned cold to the very ends of my whiskers!'

To which the Queen replied, 'You haven't got any whiskers.'

'The horror of that moment,' the King went on, 'I shall never, *never* forget!'

'You will, though,' the Queen said, 'if you don't make a memorandum of it.'

Alice looked on with great interest as the King took an enormous memorandum-book out of his pocket and began writing. A sudden thought struck her, and she took hold of the end of the pencil, which came some way over his shoulder, and began writing for him.

The poor King looked puzzled and unhappy, and struggled with the pencil for some time without saying anything; but Alice was too strong for him, and at last he panted out, 'My dear! I really *must* get a thinner pencil. I can't manage this one a bit; it writes all manner of things that I don't intend –'

'What manner of things?' said the Queen, looking over the book (in which Alice had put *The White Knight is sliding down the poker. He balances very badly*). That's not a memorandum of *your* feelings!'

There was a book lying near Alice on the table, and while she sat watching the White King (for she was still a little anxious about him, and had the ink all ready to throw over him, in case he fainted again), she turned over the leaves, to find some part that she could read, – 'for it's all in some language I don't know,' she said to herself.

It was like this:

 JABBERWOCKY

'Twas brillig, and the slithy toves
Did gyre and gimble in the wabe;
All mimsy were the borogoves,
And the mome raths outgrabe.

She puzzled over this for some time, but at last a bright thought struck her. 'Why, it's a Looking-Glass book, of course! And if I hold it up to a glass, the words will all go the right way again.'

This was the poem that Alice read:

JABBERWOCKY

> 'Twas brillig, and the slithy toves
> Did gyre and gimble in the wabe;
> All mimsy were the borogoves,
> And the mome raths outgrabe.
>
> 'Beware the Jabberwock, my son!
> The jaws that bite, the claws that catch!
> Beware the Jubjub bird and shun
> The frumious Bandersnatch!'

He took his vorpal sword in hand:
Long time the manxome foe he sought –
So rested he by the Tumtum tree,
And stood awhile in thought

And as in uffish thought he stood,
The Jabberwock, with eyes of flame,
Came whiffing through the tulgey wood,
And burbled as it came!

One, two! One, two! And through and
through
The vorpal blade went snicker-snack!
He left it dead, and with its head
He went galumphing back.

'And hast thou slain the Jabberwock!
Come to my arms, my beamish boy!
O frabjous day! Callooh! Callay!'
He chortled in his joy.

Twas brillig, and the slithy toves
Did gyre and gimble in the wabe:
All mimsy were the borogoves,
And the mome raths outgrabe.

'It seems very pretty,' she said when she had finished it, 'but it's *rather* hard to understand!' (You see she didn't like to confess even to herself, that she couldn't make it out at all.) 'Somehow it seems to fill my head with ideas – only I don't exactly know what they are! However, *somebody* killed *something*: that's clear, at any rate –

'But oh!' thought Alice, suddenly jumping up, 'if I

don't make haste I shall have to go back through the Looking-Glass, before I've seen what the rest of the house is like! Let's have a look at the garden first!' She was out of the room in a moment, and ran down stairs – or, at least, it wasn't exactly running, but a new invention for getting down stairs quickly and easily, as Alice said to herself. She just kept the tips of her fingers on the hand-rail, and floated gently down without even touching the stairs with her feet; then she floated on through the hall, and would have gone straight out at the door in the same way, if she hadn't caught hold of the doorpost. She was getting a little giddy with so much floating in the air, and was rather glad to find herself walking again in the natural way.

CHAPTER 2

The Garden of Live Flowers

'I should see the garden far better,' said Alice to herself, 'if I could get to the top of that hill: and here's a path that leads straight to it – at least, no, it doesn't do that –' (after going a few yards along the path, and turning several sharp corners), 'but I suppose it will at last. But how curiously it twists! It's more like a corkscrew than a path! Well, *this* turn goes to the hill, I suppose – no, it doesn't! This goes straight back to the house! Well, then, I'll try it the other way.'

And so she did: wandering up and down, and trying turn after turn, but always coming back to the house, do what she would. Indeed, once, when she turned a corner rather more quickly than usual, she ran against it before she could stop herself.

'It's no use talking about it,' Alice said, looking up at the house and pretending it was arguing with her. 'I'm *not* going in again yet. I know I should have to get through the Looking-Glass again – back into the old room – and there'd be an end of all my adventures!'

So, resolutely turning her back upon the house, she

set out once more down the path, determined to keep straight on till she got to the hill. For a few minutes all went on well, and she was just saying, 'I really *shall* do it this time –' when the path gave a sudden twist and shook itself (as she described it afterwards), and the next moment she found herself actually walking in at the door.

'Oh, it's too bad!' she cried. 'I never saw such a house for getting in the way! Never!'

However, there was the hill full in sight, so there was nothing to be done but start again. This time she came upon a large flower-bed, with a border of daisies, and a willow tree growing in the middle.

'O Tiger-lily,' said Alice, addressing herself to one

that was waving gracefully about in the wind, 'I *wish* you could talk!'

'We *can* talk,' said the Tiger-lily: 'when there's anybody worth talking to.'

Alice was so astonished that she couldn't speak for a minute: it quite seemed to take her breath away. At length, as the Tiger-lily only went on waving about, she spoke again, in a timid voice – almost in a whisper. 'And can *all* the flowers talk?'

'As well as *you* can,' said the Tiger-lily. 'And a great deal louder.'

'It isn't manners for us to begin, you know,' said the Rose, 'and I really was wondering when you'd speak! Said I to myself, "Her face has got *some* sense in it, though it's not a clever one!" Still, you're the right colour, and that goes a long way.'

'I don't care about the colour,' the Tiger-lily remarked. 'If only her petals curled up a little more, she'd be all right.'

Alice didn't like being criticised, so she began asking questions: 'Aren't you sometimes frightened at being planted out here, with nobody to take care of you?'

'There's the tree in the middle,' said the Rose. 'What else is it good for?'

'But what could it do, if any danger came?' Alice asked.

'It could bark,' said the Rose.

'It says "Bough-wough!"' cried a Daisy: 'that's why its branches are called boughs!'

'Didn't you know *that?*' cried another Daisy, and here they all began shouting together, till the air seemed quite full of little shrill voices. 'Silence, every one of you!' cried the Tiger-lily, waving itself passionately from side to side, and trembling with excitement. 'They know I can't get at them!' it panted, bending its quivering head towards Alice, 'or they wouldn't dare to do it!'

'Never mind!' Alice said in a soothing tone, and stooping down to the daisies, who were just beginning again, she whispered, 'If you don't hold your tongues, I'll pick you!'

There was silence in a moment, and several of the pink daisies turned white.

'That's right!' said the Tiger-lily. 'The daisies are worst of all. When one speaks, they all begin together, and it's enough to make one wither to hear the way they go on!'

'How is it you can all talk so nicely?' Alice said, hoping to get it into a better temper by a compliment. 'I've been in many gardens before, but none of the flowers could talk.'

'Put your hand down, and feel the ground,' said the Tiger-lily. 'Then you'll know why.'

Alice did so. 'It's very hard,' she said, 'but I don't see what that has to do with it.'

'In most gardens,' the Tiger-lily said, 'they make the beds too soft – so that the flowers are always asleep.'

This sounded a very good reason, and Alice was quite pleased to know it. 'I never thought of that before!' she said.

'It's *my* opinion that you never think *at all*,' the Rose said in a rather severe tone.

'I never saw anybody that looked stupider,' a Violet said, so suddenly, that Alice quite jumped; for it hadn't spoken before.

'Hold *your* tongue!' cried the Tiger-lily. 'As if *you* ever saw anybody. You keep your head under the leaves, and snore away there till you know no more what's going on in the world, than if you were a bud!'

'Are there any more people in the garden besides me?' Alice said, not choosing to notice the Rose's last remark.

'There's one other flower in the garden that can move about like you,' said the Rose. 'I wonder how you do it –' ('You're always wondering,' said the Tiger-lily), 'but she's more bushy than you are.'

'Is she like me?' Alice asked eagerly, for the thought crossed her mind, 'There's another little girl in the garden somewhere!'

'Well, she has the same awkward shape as you,' the Rose said: 'but she's redder – and her petals are shorter, I think.'

'They're done up close, like a dahlia, 'said the Tiger-lily: 'not tumbled about, like yours.'

'But that's not *your* fault,' the Rose added kindly: 'you're beginning to fade, you know – and then one can't help one's petals getting a little untidy.'

Alice didn't like this idea at all: so, to change the subject, she asked, 'Does she ever come out here?'

'I dare say you'll see her soon,' said the Rose. 'She's one of the kind that has nine spikes, you know.'

'Where does she wear them?' Alice asked, with some curiosity.

'Why, all round her head, of course,' the Rose replied. 'I was wondering *you* hadn't got some too. I thought it was the regular rule.'

'She's coming!' cried the Larkspur. 'I hear her footstep, thump, thump, along the gravel-walk!'

Alice looked round eagerly, and found that it was the Red Queen. 'She's grown a good deal!' was her first remark. She had indeed; when Alice first found her in the ashes, she had been only three inches high – and here she was, half a head taller than Alice herself!

'It's the fresh air that does it,' said the Rose: 'wonderfully fine air it is, out here.'

'I think I'll go and meet her,' said Alice, for, though the flowers were interesting enough, she felt that it would be far grander to have a talk with a real Queen.

'You can't possibly do that,' said the Rose: '*I* should advise you to walk the other way.'

This sounded nonsense to Alice, so she said nothing, but set off at once towards the Red Queen. To her surprise, she lost sight of her in a moment, and found herself walking in at the front-door again.

A little provoked, she drew back, and, after looking everywhere for the Queen (whom she spied out at last, a long way off), she thought she would try the plan, this time, of walking in the opposite direction.

It succeeded beautifully. She had not been walking a minute before she found herself face to face with the Red Queen, and full in sight of the hill she had been so long aiming at.

'Where do you come from?' said the Red Queen. 'And where are you going? Look up, speak nicely, and don't twiddle your fingers all the time.'

Alice attended to all these directions, and explained, as well as she could, that she had lost her way.

'I don't know what you mean by *your* way,' said the Queen: 'all the ways about here belong to *me* – but why did you come out here at all?' she added in a kinder tone. 'Curtsey while you're thinking what to say. It saves time.'

Alice wondered a little at this, but she was too much in awe of the Queen to disbelieve it. 'I'll try it when I

go home,' she thought to herself, 'the next time I'm a little late for dinner.'

'It's time for you to answer now,' the Queen said, looking at her watch: 'open your mouth a *little* wider when you speak, and always say "your Majesty."'

'I only wanted to see what the garden was like, your Majesty –'

'That's right,' said the Queen, patting her on the head, which Alice didn't like at all: 'though, when you say "garden," *I've* seen gardens, compared with which this would be a wilderness.'

Alice didn't care to argue the point, but went on: '– and I thought I'd try and find my way to the top of that hill –'

'When you say "hill,"' the Queen interrupted, '*I*

could show you hills, in comparison with which you'd call that a valley.'

'No, I shouldn't,' said Alice, surprised into contradicting her at last: 'a hill *can't* be a valley, you know. That would be nonsense –'

The Red Queen shook her head. 'You may call it "nonsense" if you like,' she said, 'but *I've* heard nonsense, compared with which that would be as sensible as a dictionary!'

Alice curtseyed again, as she was afraid from the Queen's tone that she was a *little* offended: and they walked on in silence till they got to the top of the little hill.

For some minutes Alice stood without speaking, looking out in all directions over the country – and a most curious country it was. There were a number of tiny little brooks running straight across it from side to side, and the ground between was divided up into squares by a number of little green hedges, that reached from brook to brook.

'I declare it's marked out just like a large chessboard!' Alice said at last. 'There ought to be some men moving about somewhere – and so there are!' she added in a tone of delight, and her heart began to beat quick with excitement as she went on. 'It's a great huge game of chess that's being played – all over the world – if this *is* the world at all, you know. Oh, what fun it is! How I *wish* I was one of them! I wouldn't mind being a Pawn, if only I might join – though, of course, I should *like* to be a Queen, best.'

She glanced rather shyly at the real Queen as she said this, but her companion only smiled pleasantly, and said, 'That's easily managed. You can be the White Queen's

Pawn, if you like, as Lily's too young to play; and you're in the Second Square to begin with: when you get to the Eighth Square you'll be a Queen –' Just at this moment, somehow or other, they began to run.

Alice never could quite make out, in thinking it over afterwards, how it was that they began: all she remembers is that they were running hand in hand, and the Queen went so fast that it was all she could do to keep up with her: and still the Queen kept crying, 'Faster! Faster!' but Alice felt she *could not* go faster, though she had no breath left to say so.

The most curious part of the thing was, that the trees and the other things round them never changed their places at all: however fast they went, they never seemed to pass anything. 'I wonder if all the things move along with us?' thought poor puzzled Alice. And the Queen seemed to guess her thoughts, for she cried, 'Faster! Don't try to talk!'

Not that Alice had any idea of doing *that*. She felt as if she would never be able to talk again, she was getting so out of breath: and still the Queen cried, 'Faster! Faster!'

and dragged her along. 'Are we nearly there?' Alice managed to pant out at last.

'Nearly there!' the Queen repeated. 'Why, we passed it ten minutes ago! Faster!' And then ran on for a time in silence, with the wind whistling in Alice's ears, and almost blowing her hair off her head, she fancied.

'Now! Now!' cried the Queen. 'Faster! Faster!' And they went so fast that at last they seemed to skim through the air, hardly touching the ground with their feet, till suddenly, just as Alice was getting quite exhausted, they stopped, and she found herself sitting on the ground breathless and giddy.

The Queen propped her up against a tree, and said kindly, 'You may rest a little now.'

Alice looked round her in great surprise. 'Why, I do believe we've been under this tree the whole time! Everything's just as it was!'

'Of course it is,' said the Queen: 'what would you have it?'

'Well, in *our* country,' said Alice, still panting a little, 'you'd generally get to somewhere else – if you ran very fast for a long time, as we've been doing.'

'A slow sort of country!' said the Queen. 'Now *here*, you see, it takes all the running *you* can do, to keep in the same place. If you want to get somewhere else, you must run at least twice as fast as that!'

'I'd rather not try, please!' said Alice. 'I'm quite content to stay here – only I *am* so hot and thirsty!'

'I know what *you'd* like!' the Queen said good-naturedly, taking a little box out of her pocket. 'Have a biscuit?'

Alice thought it would not be civil to say 'No,' though it wasn't at all what she wanted. So she took it, and ate it as well as she could: and it was *very* dry; and she thought she had never been so nearly choked in all her life.

'While you're refreshing yourself,' said the Queen, 'I'll just take the measurements.' And she took a ribbon out of her pocket, marked in inches, and began measuring the ground, and sticking little pegs in here and there.

'At the end of two yards,' she said, putting in a peg to mark the distance, 'I shall give you your directions – have another biscuit?'

'No, thank you,' said Alice: 'one's *quite* enough!'

'Thirst quenched, I hope?' said the Queen.

Alice did not know what to say to this, but luckily the Queen did not wait for an answer, but went on. 'At the end of *three* yards I shall repeat them – for fear of your forgetting them. At the end of *four*, I shall say goodbye. And at the end of *five*, I shall go!'

She had got all the pegs put in by this time, and Alice looked on with great interest as she returned to the tree, and then began slowly walking down the row.

At the two-yard peg she faced round, and said, 'A pawn goes two squares in its first move, you know. So you'll go *very* quickly through the Third Square – by railway, I should think – and you'll find yourself in the Fourth Square in no time. Well, *that* square belongs to Tweedledum and Tweedledee – the Fifth is mostly water – the sixth belongs to Humpty Dumpty – But you make no remark?'

'I – I didn't know I had to make one – just then,' Alice faltered out.

'You *should* have said,' the Queen went on in a tone of grave reproof, '"It's extremely kind of you to tell me

all this" – however, we'll suppose it said – the Seventh Square is all forest – however, one of the Knights will show you the way – and in the Eighth Square we shall be Queens together, and it's all feasting and fun!' Alice got up and curtseyed, and sat down again.

At the next peg the Queen turned again, and this time she said, 'Speak in French when you can't think of the English for a thing – turn out your toes as you walk – and remember who you are!' She did not wait for Alice to curtsey this time, but walked on quickly to the next peg, where she turned for a moment to say 'goodbye,' and then hurried on to the last.

How it happened Alice never knew, but exactly as she came to the last peg, she was gone. Whether she vanished into the air, or whether she ran quickly into the wood ('and she *can* run very fast!' thought Alice), there was no way of guessing, but she was gone, and Alice began to remember that she was a Pawn, and that it would soon be time for her to move.

CHAPTER 3

Looking-Glass Insects

Of course the first thing to do was to make a grand survey of the country she was going to travel through. 'It's something very like learning geography,' thought Alice, as she stood on tiptoe in hopes of being able to see a little farther. 'Principal rivers – there *are* none. Principal mountains – I'm on the only one, but I don't think it's got any name. Principal towns – why, what *are* those creatures, making honey down there? They can't be bees – nobody ever saw bees a mile off, you know –' and for some time she stood silent, watching one of them that was bustling about among the flowers, poking its proboscis into them 'just as if it was a regular bee,' thought Alice.

However, this was anything but a regular bee: in fact, it was an elephant – as Alice soon found out, though the idea quite took her breath away at first. 'And what enormous flowers they must be!' was her next idea. 'Something like cottages with the roofs taken off, and stalks put to them – and what quantities of honey they must make! I think I'll go down and – no, I won't go *just* yet,' she went on, checking herself just as she was beginning to run down the hill, and trying to find some excuse for turning shy so suddenly. 'It'll never do to go down among them without a good long branch to brush them away – and what fun it'll be when they ask me how I liked my walk. I shall say – "Oh, I liked it well enough – " (here came the favourite little toss of the head), "only it was so dusty and hot, and the elephants did tease so!"

'I think I'll go down the other way,' she said, after a pause: 'and perhaps I may visit the elephants later on. Besides, I do so want to get into the Third Square!'

So with this excuse she ran down the hill and jumped over the first of the six little brooks.

'Tickets, please!' said the Guard, putting his head in at the window. In a moment everybody was holding out a ticket: they were about the same size as the people, and quite seemed to fill the carriage.

'Now then! Show your ticket, child!' the Guard went on, looking angrily at Alice. And a great many voices all said together ('like the chorus of a song,' thought Alice), 'Don't keep him waiting, child! Why, his time is worth a thousand pounds a minute!'

'I'm afraid I haven't got one,' Alice said in a frightened tone: 'there wasn't a ticket-office where I came from.' And again the chorus of voices went on. 'There wasn't room for one where she came from. The land there is worth a thousand pounds an inch!'

'Don't make excuses,' said the Guard: 'you should have bought one from the engine-driver.' And once more the chorus of voices went on with 'The man that drives the engine. Why, the smoke alone is worth a thousand pounds a puff!'

Alice thought to herself, 'Then there's no use in speaking.' The voices didn't join in this time, as she hadn't spoken, but, to her great surprise, they all *thought* in chorus (I hope you understand what *thinking in chorus* means – for I must confess that *I* don't), 'Better say nothing at all. Language is worth a thousand pounds a word!'

'I shall dream about a thousand pounds tonight, I know I shall!' thought Alice.

All this time the Guard was looking at her, first through a telescope, then through a microscope, and then through an opera-glass. At last he said, 'You're travelling the wrong way,' and shut up the window and went away.

'So young a child,' said the gentleman sitting opposite to her (he was dressed in white paper), 'ought to know which way she's going, even if she doesn't know her own name!'

A Goat, that was sitting next to the gentleman in white, shut his eyes and said in a loud voice, 'She ought to know her way to the ticket-office, even if she doesn't know her alphabet!'

There was a Beetle sitting next the Goat (it was a very queer carriage-full of passengers altogether), and as the rule seemed to be that they should all speak in turn, *he* went on with 'She'll have to go back from here as luggage!'

Alice couldn't see who was sitting beyond the Beetle, but a hoarse voice spoke next. 'Change engines –' it said, and there it choked and was obliged to leave off.

'It sounds like a horse,' Alice thought to herself. And an extremely small voice, close to her ear, said 'you might make a joke on that – something about "horse" and "hoarse," you know.'

Then a very gentle voice in the distance said, 'She must be labelled "Lass, with care," you know –'

And after that other voices went on ('What a number of people there are in the carriage!' thought Alice), saying 'She must go by post, as she's got a head on her –' 'She must be sent as a message by the telegraph –' 'She must draw the train herself the rest of the way –,' and so on.

But the gentleman dressed in white paper leaned forwards and whispered in her ear, 'Never mind what they all say, my dear, but take a return-ticket every time the train stops.'

'Indeed I shan't!' Alice said rather impatiently. 'I don't belong to this railway journey at all – I was in a wood just now – and I wish I could get back there!'

'You might make a joke on *that*.' said the little voice close to her ear: 'something about you *would* if you could, you know.'

'Don't tease so,' said Alice, looking about in vain to

see where the voice came from; 'if you're so anxious to have a joke made, why don't you make one yourself?'

The little voice sighed deeply: it was *very* unhappy evidently, and Alice would have said something pitying to comfort it, 'if it would only sigh like other people!' she thought. But this was such a wonderfully small sigh, that she wouldn't have heard it at all, if it hadn't come *quite* close to her ear. The consequence of this was that it tickled her ear very much, and quite took off her thoughts from the unhappiness of the poor little creature.

'I know you are a friend,' the little voice went on; 'a dear friend, and an old friend. And you won't hurt me though I *am* an insect.'

'What kind of insect?' Alice inquired a little anxiously. What she really wanted to know was, whether it could sting or not, but she thought this wouldn't be quite a civil question to ask.

'What, then you don't –' the little voice began, when it was drowned by a shrill scream from the engine, and everybody jumped up in alarm, Alice among the rest.

The Horse, who had put his head out of the window, quickly drew it in and said, 'It's only a brook we have to jump over.' Everybody seemed satisfied with this, though Alice felt a little nervous at the idea of trains jumping at all. 'However, it will take us into the Fourth Square, that's some comfort!' she said to herself. In another moment she felt the carriage rise straight up into the air, and in her fright she caught at the thing nearest to her hand, which happened to be the Goat's beard.

But the beard seemed to melt away as she touched it, and she found herself sitting quietly under a tree – while the Gnat (for that was the insect she had been talking to) was balancing itself on a twig just over her head, and fanning her with its wings.

It certainly was a *very* large Gnat: 'about the size of a chicken,' Alice thought. Still, she couldn't feel nervous with it, after they had been talking together so long.

'– then you don't like all insects?' the Gnat went on, as quietly as if nothing had happened.

'I like them when they can talk,' Alice said. 'None of them ever talk, where *I* come from.'

'What sort of insects do you rejoice in, where *you* come from?' the Gnat inquired.

'I don't *rejoice* in insects at all,' Alice explained, 'because I'm rather afraid of them – at least the large kinds. But I can tell you the names of some of them.'

'Of course they answer to their names?' the Gnat remarked carelessly.

'I never knew them do it.'

'What's the use of their having names,' the Gnat said, 'if they won't answer to them?'

'No use to *them*,' said Alice; 'but it's useful to the people that name them, I suppose. If not, why do things have names at all?'

'I can't say,' the Gnat replied. 'Farther on in the wood down there, they've got no names – however, go on with your list of insects: you're wasting time.'

'Well, there's the Horse-fly,' Alice began, counting off the names on her fingers.

'All right,' said the Gnat: 'half way up that bush, you'll see a Rocking-horse-fly, if you look. It's made entirely of wood, and gets about by swinging itself from branch to branch.'

'What does it live on?' Alice asked with great curiosity.

'Sap and sawdust,' said the Gnat. 'Go on with the list.'

Alice looked at the Rocking-horse-fly with great interest, and made up her mind that it must have been just repainted, it looked so bright and sticky; and then she went on:

'And there's the Dragon-fly.'

'Look on the branch above your head,' said the Gnat, 'and there you'll find a Snap-dragon-fly. Its body is made of plum-pudding, its wings of holly-leaves, and its head is a raisin burning in brandy.'

'And what does it live on?' Alice asked, as before.

'Frumenty and mince-pie,' the Gnat replied: 'and it makes its nest in a Christmas-box.'

'And then there's the Butterfly,' Alice went on, after she had taken a good look at the insect with its head on fire, and had thought to herself, 'I wonder if that's the reason insects are so fond of flying into candles – because they want to turn into Snap-dragon-flies!'

'Crawling at your feet,' said the Gnat (Alice drew her feet back in some alarm), 'you may observe a Bread-and-butter-fly. Its wings are thin slices of bread-and-butter, its body is a crust, and its head is a lump of sugar.'

'And what does *it* live on?'

'Weak tea with cream in it.'

A new difficulty came into Alice's head. 'Supposing it couldn't find any?' she suggested.

'Then it would die, of course.'

'But that must happen very often,' Alice remarked thoughtfully.

'It always happens,' said the Gnat.

After this, Alice was silent for a minute or two, pondering. The Gnat amused itself meanwhile by humming round and round her head: at last it settled again and remarked, 'I suppose you don't want to lose your name?'

'No, indeed,' Alice said, a little anxiously.

'And yet I don't know,' the Gnat went on in a careless tone: 'only think how convenient it would be if you could manage to go home without it! For instance, if the governess wanted to call you to your lessons, she would call out "Come here –," and there she would have to leave off, because there wouldn't be any name for her to call, and of course you wouldn't have to go, you know.'

'That would never do, I'm sure,' said Alice: 'the

governess would never think of excusing me lessons for that. If she couldn't remember my name, she'd call me "Miss!" as the servants do.'

'Well, if she said "Miss," and didn't say anything more,' the Gnat remarked, 'of course you'd miss your lessons. That's a joke. I wish *you* had made it.'

'Why do you wish *I* had made it?' Alice asked. 'It's a very bad one.'

But the Gnat only sighed deeply, while two large tears came rolling down its cheeks.

'You shouldn't make jokes,' Alice said, 'if it makes you so unhappy.'

Then came another of those melancholy little sighs, and this time the poor Gnat really seemed to have sighed itself away, for, when Alice looked up, there was nothing whatever to be seen on the twig, and, as she was getting quite chilly, with sitting still so long, she got up and walked on.

She very soon came to an open field, with a wood on the other side of it: it looked much darker than the last wood, and Alice felt a *little* timid about going into it. However, on second thoughts, she made up her mind to go on: 'for I certainly won't go *back*,' she thought to herself, and this was the only way to the Eighth Square.

'This must be the wood,' she said thoughtfully to herself, 'where things have no names. I wonder what'll become of *my* name when I go in? I shouldn't like to lose it at all – because they'd have to give me another, and it would be almost certain to be an ugly one. But then the fun would be, trying to find the creature that had got my old name! That's just like the advertisements, you know, when people lose dogs – "*answers to the name of 'Dash': had on a brass collar*" – just fancy calling everything you met "Alice," till one of them answered! Only they wouldn't answer at all, if they were wise.'

She was rambling on in this way when she reached the wood: it looked very cool and shady. 'Well, at any rate it's a great comfort,' she said, as she stepped under the trees, 'after being so hot, to get into the – into the – into *what?*' she went on, rather surprised at not being able to think of the word. 'I mean to get under the – under the – under *this*, you know!' putting her hand on the trunk of the tree. 'What *does* it call itself, I wonder? I do believe it's got no name – why, to be sure it hasn't!'

She stood silent for a minute thinking: then she suddenly began again. 'Then it really *has* happened, after all! And now, who am I? I *will* remember, if I can! I'm determined to do it!' But being determined didn't help her much, and all she could say, after a great deal of puzzling, was, 'L, I *know* it begins with L!'

Just then a Fawn came wandering by: it looked at Alice with its large gentle eyes, but didn't seem at all frightened.

'Here then! Here then!' Alice said, as she held out

her hand and tried to stroke it; but it only started back a little, and then stood looking at her again.

'What do you call yourself?' the Fawn said at last. Such a soft sweet voice it had!

'I wish I knew!' thought poor Alice. She answered, rather sadly, 'Nothing just now.'

'Think again,' it said: 'that won't do.'

Alice thought, but nothing came of it. 'Please, would you tell me what *you* call yourself?' she said timidly. 'I think that might help a little.'

'I'll tell you, if you'll come a little farther on,' the Fawn said. 'I can't remember here.'

So they walked on together through the wood, Alice with her arms clasped lovingly round the soft neck of the Fawn, till they came out into another open field, and there the Fawn gave a sudden bound into the air, and shook itself free from Alice's arm. 'I'm a Fawn!' it cried out in a voice of delight. 'And, dear me! you're a human child!' A sudden look of alarm came into its beautiful brown eyes, and in another moment it had darted away at full speed.

Alice stood looking after it, almost ready to cry with vexation at having lost her dear little fellow-traveller so suddenly. 'However, I know my name now,' she said: 'that's some comfort. Alice – Alice – I won't forget it again. And now, which of these finger-posts ought I to follow, I wonder?'

It was not a very difficult question to answer, as there was only one road through the wood, and the two fingerposts both pointed along it. 'I'll settle it,' Alice said to herself, 'when the road divides and they point different ways.'

But this did not seem likely to happen. She went on and on, a long way, but wherever the road divided there was sure to be two fingerposts pointing the same way, one marked 'TO TWEEDLEDUM'S HOUSE,' and the other 'TO THE HOUSE OF TWEEDLEDEE.'

'I do believe,' said Alice at last, 'that they live in the same house! I wonder I never thought of that before – But I can't stay there long. I'll just call and say, "How d'ye do?" and ask them the way out of the wood. If I could only get to the Eighth Square before it gets dark!' So she wandered on, talking to herself as she went, till, on turning a sharp corner, she came upon two fat little men, so suddenly that she could not help starting back, but in another moment she recovered herself, feeling sure that they must be Tweedledum and Tweedledee.

CHAPTER 4

Tweedledum and Tweedledee

They were standing under a tree, each with an arm round the other's neck, and Alice knew which was which in a moment, because one of them had DUM embroidered on his collar, and the other DEE. 'I suppose they've each got TWEEDLE round at the back of the collar,' she said to herself.

They stood so still that she quite forgot they were alive, and she was just going round to see if the word TWEEDLE was written at the back of each collar, when she was startled by a voice coming from the one marked DUM.

'If you think we're waxworks,' he said, 'you ought to pay, you know. Waxworks weren't made to be looked at for nothing. Nohow!'

'Contrariwise,' added the one marked DEE, 'if you think we're alive, you ought to speak.'

'I'm sure I'm very sorry,' was all Alice could say; for the words of the old song kept ringing through her head like the ticking of a clock, and she could hardly help saying them out loud:

Tweedledum and Tweedledee
Agreed to have a battle;
For Tweedledum said Tweedledee
Had spoiled his nice new rattle.

Just then flew down a monstrous crow,
As black as a tar-barrel;
Which frightened both the heroes so,
They quite forgot their quarrel.

'I know what you're thinking about,' said Tweedledum: 'but it isn't so, nohow.'

'Contrariwise,' continued Tweedledee, 'if it was so, it might be; and if it were so, it would be: but as it isn't, it ain't. That's logic.'

'I was thinking,' Alice said very politely, 'which is the best way out of this wood: it's getting so dark. Would you tell me please?'

But the fat little men only looked at each other and grinned.

They looked so exactly like a couple of great school-boys, that Alice couldn't help pointing her finger at Tweedledum, and saying 'First Boy!'

'Nohow!' Tweedledum cried out briskly, and shut his mouth up again with a snap.

'Next Boy!' said Alice, passing on to Tweedledee, though she felt quite certain he would only shout out 'Contrariwise!' and so he did.

'You've begun wrong!' cried Tweedledum. 'The first thing in a visit is to say "How d'ye do?" and shake hands!' And here the two brothers gave each other a hug, and then they held out the two hands that were free, to shake hands with her.

Alice did not like shaking hands with either of them first, for fear of hurting the other one's feelings; so, as the best way out of the difficulty, she took hold of both hands at once: the next moment they were dancing round in a ring. This seemed quite natural (she remembered afterwards), and she was not even surprised to hear music playing: it seemed to come from the tree under which they were dancing, and it was done (as well as she could make it out) by the branches rubbing one across the other, like fiddles and fiddlesticks.

'But it certainly *was* funny' (Alice said afterwards, when she was telling her sister the history of all this) 'to find myself singing "*Here we go round the mulberry bush.*" I don't know when I began it, but somehow I felt as if I'd been singing it a long, long time!'

The other two dancers were fat, and very soon out of breath. 'Four times round is enough for one dance,' Tweedledum panted out, and they left off dancing as suddenly as they had begun: the music stopped at the same moment.

Then they let go of Alice's hands, and stood looking at her for a minute: there was a rather awkward pause, as Alice didn't know how to begin a conversation with people she had just been dancing with. 'It would never do to say, "How d'ye do?" *now*,' she said to herself: 'we seem to have got beyond that, somehow!'

'I hope you're not much tired?' she said at last.

'Nohow. And thank you *very* much for asking,' said Tweedledum.

'So *much* obliged!' added Tweedledee. 'You like poetry?'

'Ye-es, pretty well – *some* poetry,' Alice said doubtfully. 'Would you tell me which road leads out of the wood?'

'What shall I repeat to her?' said Tweedledee, looking round at Tweedledum with great solemn eyes, and not noticing Alice's question.

'"*The Walrus and the Carpenter*" is the longest,' Tweedledum replied, giving his brother an affectionate hug.

Tweedledee began instantly –

'The sun was shining –'

Here Alice ventured to interrupt him. 'If it's *very* long,' she said, as politely as she could, 'would you please tell me first which road –'

Tweedledee smiled gently, and began again:

> *The sun was shining on the sea,*
> *Shining with all his might:*
> *He did his very best to make*
> *The billows smooth and bright –*

And this was odd, because it was
The middle of the night.

The moon was shining sulkily,
Because she thought the sun
Had got no business to be there
After the day was done –
"It's very rude of him," she said,
"To come and spoil the fun!"

The sea was wet as wet could be,
The sands were dry as dry.
You could not see a cloud, because
No cloud was in the sky:
No birds were flying overhead –
There were no birds to fly.

The Walrus and the Carpenter Were
walking close at hand:
They wept like anything to see
Such quantities of sand

"If this were only cleared away,"
They said, "it would be grand!"

"If seven maids with seven mops
Swept it for half a year,
Do you suppose," the Walrus said,
"That they could get it clear?"
"I doubt it," said the Carpenter,
And shed a bitter tear.

"O Oysters, come and walk with us!"
The Walrus did beseech.
"A pleasant walk, a pleasant talk,
Along the briny beach:
We cannot do with more than four
To give a hand to each."

The eldest Oyster looked at him,
But never a word he said:
The eldest Oyster winked his eye,
And shook his heavy head –
Meaning to say he did not choose
To leave the oyster-bed.

But four young Oysters hurried up,
All eager for the treat:
Their coats were brushed, their faces washed,
Their shoes were clean and neat –
And this was odd, because, you know,
They hadn't any feet.

Four other Oysters followed them,
And yet another four;

And thick and fast they came at last,
And more, and more, and more –
All hopping through the frothy waves,
And scrambling to the shore.

The Walrus and the Carpenter
Walked on a mile or so,
And then they rested on a rock
Conveniently low:
And all the little Oysters stood
And waited in a row.

"The time has come," the
Walrus said, "To talk of many things:
Of shoes – and ships – and sealing-wax –
Of cabbages – and kings –
And why the sea is boiling hot –
And whether pigs have wings."

"But wait a bit," the Oysters cried,
"Before we have our chat;

For some of us are out of breath,
And all of us are fat!"
"No hurry!" said the Carpenter.
They thanked him much for that.

"A loaf of bread," the Walrus said,
"Is what we chiefly need:
Pepper and vinegar besides
Are very good indeed –
Now, if you're ready, Oysters dear,
We can begin to feed."

"But not on us!" the Oysters cried,
Turning a little blue.
"After such kindness, that would be
A dismal thing to do!"
"The night is fine," the Walrus said.
"Do you admire the view?

"It was so kind of you to come!
And you are very nice!"

The Carpenter said nothing but
"Cut us another slice.
I wish you were not quite so deaf –
I've had to ask you twice!"

"It seems a shame," the Walrus said,
"To play them such a trick.
After we've brought them out so far,
And made them trot so quick!"
The Carpenter said nothing but
"The butter's spread too thick!"

"I weep for you," the Walrus said:
"I deeply sympathise."
With sobs and tears he sorted out
Those of the largest size,
Holding his pocket-handkerchief
Before his streaming eyes.

"O Oysters," said the Carpenter,
"You've had a pleasant run!
Shall we be trotting home again!"
But answer came there none –
And this was scarcely odd, because
They'd eaten every one.?

'I like the Walrus best,' said Alice: 'because he was a little sorry for the poor oysters.'

'He ate more than the Carpenter, though,' said Tweedledee. 'You see he held his handkerchief in front, so that the Carpenter couldn't count how many he took: contrariwise.'

'That was mean!' Alice said indignantly. 'Then I like

the Carpenter best – if he didn't eat so many as the Walrus.'

'But he ate as many as he could get,' said Tweedledum.

This was a puzzler. After a pause, Alice began, 'Well! They were *both* very unpleasant characters –' Here she checked herself in some alarm, at hearing something that sounded to her like the puffing of a large steam-engine in the wood near them, though she feared it was more likely to be a wild beast. 'Are there any lions or tigers about here?' she asked timidly.

'It's only the Red King snoring,' said Tweedledee.

'Come and look at him!' the brothers cried, and they each took one of Alice's hands, and led her up to where the King was sleeping.

'Isn't he a *lovely* sight?' said Tweedledum.

Alice couldn't say honestly that he was. He had a tall red nightcap on, with a tassel, and he was lying crumpled up into a sort of untidy heap, and snoring loud – 'fit to snore his head off!' as Tweedledum remarked.

'I'm afraid he'll catch cold with lying on the damp grass,' said Alice, who was a very thoughtful little girl.

'He's dreaming now,' said Tweedledee: 'and what do you think he's dreaming about?'

Alice said, 'Nobody can guess that.'

'Why, about *you!*' Tweedledee exclaimed, clapping his hands triumphantly. 'And if he left off dreaming about you, where do you suppose you'd be?'

'Where I am now, of course,' said Alice.

'Not you!' Tweedledee retorted contemptuously. 'You'd be nowhere. Why, you're only a sort of thing in his dream!'

'If that there King was to wake,' added Tweedledum, 'you'd go out – bang! – just like a candle!'

I shouldn't!' Alice exclaimed indignantly. 'Besides, if *I'm* only a sort of thing in his dream, what are *you*, I should like to know?'

'Ditto,' said Tweedledum.

'Ditto, ditto,' cried Tweedledee.

He shouted this so loud that Alice couldn't help saying, 'Hush! You'll be waking him, I'm afraid, if you make so much noise.'

'Well, it's no use *your* talking about waking him,' said Tweedledum, 'when you're only one of the things in his dream. You know very well you're not real.'

'I *am* real!' said Alice, and began to cry.

'You won't make yourself a bit realler by crying,' Tweedledee remarked: 'there's nothing to cry about.'

'If I wasn't real,' Alice said – half-laughing through her tears, it all seemed so ridiculous – 'I shouldn't be able to cry.'

'I hope you don't suppose those are *real* tears?' Tweedledum interrupted in a tone of great contempt.

'I know they're talking nonsense,' Alice thought to herself: 'and it's foolish to cry about it.' So she brushed away her tears, and went on, as cheerfully as she could, 'At any rate I'd better be getting out of the wood, for really it's coming on very dark. Do you think it's going to rain?'

Tweedledum spread a large umbrella over himself and his brother, and looked up into it. 'No, I don't think it is,' he said: 'at least – not under *here*. Nohow.'

'But it may rain *outside?*'

'It may – if it chooses,' said Tweedledee: 'we've no objection. Contrariwise.'

'Selfish things!' thought Alice, and she was just going to say 'Good-night' and leave them, when Tweedledum sprang out from under the umbrella, and seized her by the wrist.

'Do you see *that?*' he said, in a voice choking with passion and his eyes grew large and yellow all in a moment, as he pointed with a trembling finger at a small white thing lying under the tree.

'It's only a rattle,' Alice said, after a careful examination of the little white thing. 'Not a rattle-*snake*, you know,' she added hastily, thinking that he was frightened: 'only an old rattle – quite old and broken.'

'I knew it was!' cried Tweedledum, beginning to stamp about wildly and tear his hair. 'It's spoilt, of course!' Here he looked at Tweedledee, who immediately sat down on the ground, and tried to hide himself under the umbrella.

Alice laid her hand upon his arm, and said, in a soothing tone, 'You needn't be so angry about an old rattle.'

'But it *isn't* old!' Tweedledum cried, in a greater

fury than ever. 'It's new, I tell you – I bought it yesterday – my nice *new* RATTLE!' and his voice rose to a perfect scream.

All this time Tweedledee was trying his best to fold up the umbrella, with himself in it: which was such an extraordinary thing to do, that it quite took off Alice's attention from the angry brother. But he couldn't quite succeed, and it ended in his rolling over, bundled up in the umbrella, with only his head out: and there he lay, opening and shutting his mouth and his large eyes – 'looking more like a fish than anything else,' Alice thought.

'Of course you agree to have a battle?' Tweedledum said in a calmer tone.

'I suppose so,' the other sulkily replied, as he crawled out of the umbrella: 'only *she* must help us to dress up, you know.'

So the two brothers went off hand-in-hand into the wood, and returned in a minute with their arms full of things – such as bolsters, blankets, hearth-rugs, table-cloths, dish-covers, and coal-scuttles. 'I hope you're a good hand at pinning and tying strings?' Tweedledum remarked. 'Every one of these things has got to go on, somehow or other.'

Alice said afterwards she had never seen such a fuss made about anything in all her life – the way those two bustled about – and the quantity of things they put on – and the trouble they gave her in tying strings and fastening buttons – 'Really they'll be more like bundles of old clothes than anything else, by the time they're ready!' she said to herself, as she arranged a bolster round the neck of Tweedledee, 'to keep his head from being cut off,' as he said.

'You know,' he added very gravely, 'it's one of the most serious things that can possibly happen to one in a battle – to get one's head cut off.'

Alice laughed loud; but she managed to turn it into a cough, for fear of hurting his feelings.

'Do I look very pale?' said Tweedledum, coming up to have his helmet tied on. (He *called* it a helmet, though it certainly looked much more like a saucepan.)

'Well – yes – a *little*,' Alice replied gently.

'I'm very brave, generally,' he went on in a low voice: 'only to-day I happen to have a headache.'

'And *I've* got a toothache!' said Tweedledee, who had overheard the remark. 'I'm far worse than you!'

'Then you'd better not fight today,' said Alice, thinking it a good opportunity to make peace.

'We *must* have a bit of a fight, but I don't care about going on long,' said Tweedledum. 'What's the time now?'

Tweedledee looked at his watch, and said, 'Half-past four.'

'Let's fight till six, and then have dinner,' said Tweedledum.

'Very well,' the other said, rather sadly: 'and *she* can watch us – only you'd better not come *very* close,' he added: 'I generally hit everything I can see – when I get really excited.'

'And *I* hit everything within reach,' cried Tweedledum, 'whether I can see it or not!'

Alice laughed. 'You must hit the *trees* pretty often, I should think,' she said.

Tweedledum looked round him with a satisfied smile. 'I don't suppose,' he said, 'there'll be a tree left standing, for ever so far round, by the time we've finished!'

'And all about a rattle!' said Alice, still hoping to make them a *little* ashamed of fighting for such a trifle.

'I shouldn't have minded it so much,' said Tweedledum, 'if it hadn't been a new one.'

'I wish the monstrous crow would come!' thought Alice.

'There's only one sword, you know,' Tweedledum said to his brother: 'but you can have the umbrella – it's quite as sharp. Only we must begin quick. It's getting as dark as it can.'

'And darker,' said Tweedledee.

It was getting dark so suddenly that Alice thought there must be a thunderstorm coming on. 'What a thick black cloud that is!' she said. 'And how fast it comes! Why, I do believe it's got wings!'

'It's the crow!' Tweedledum cried out in a shrill voice of alarm; and the two brothers took to their heels and were out of sight in a moment.

Alice ran a little way into the wood and stopped under a large tree.

'It can never get at me *here*,' she thought; 'it's far too large to squeeze itself in among the trees. But I wish it wouldn't flap its wings so – it makes quite a hurricane in the wood – here's somebody's shawl being blown away!'

CHAPTER 5

Wool and Water

She caught the shawl as she spoke, and looked about for the owner: in another moment the White Queen came running wildly through the wood, with both arms stretched out wide, as if she were flying, and Alice very civilly went to meet her with the shawl.

'I'm very glad I happened to be in the way,' Alice said, as she helped her to put on her shawl again.

The White Queen only looked at her in a helpless, frightened sort of way, and kept repeating something in a whisper to herself that sounded like 'Bread-and-butter, bread-and-butter,' and Alice felt that if there was to be any conversation at all, she must manage it herself. So she began rather timidly: 'Am I addressing the White Queen?'

'Well, yes, if you call that a-dressing,' the Queen said. 'It isn't *my* notion of the thing at all.'

Alice thought it would never do to have an argument at the very beginning of their conversation, so she smiled and said, 'If your Majesty will only tell me the right way to begin, I'll do it as well as I can.'

'But I don't want it done at all!' groaned the poor Queen. 'I've been a-dressing myself for the last two hours.'

It would have been all the better, as it seemed to Alice, if she had got some one else to dress her, she was so dreadfully untidy. 'Every single thing's crooked,' Alice thought to herself, 'and she's all over pins! – May I put your shawl straight for you?' she added aloud.

'I don't know what's the matter with it!' the Queen said in a melancholy voice. 'It's out of temper, I think. I've pinned it here, and I've pinned it there, but there's no pleasing it!'

'It *can't* go straight, you know, if you pin it all on one side,' Alice said, as she gently put it right for her; 'and, dear me, what a state your hair is in!'

'The brush has got entangled in it!' the Queen said with a sigh. 'And I lost the comb yesterday.'

Alice carefully released the brush, and did her best to get the hair into order. 'Come, you look rather better now!' she said, after altering most of the pins. 'But really you should have a lady's-maid!'

'I'm sure I'll take *you* with pleasure!' the Queen said. 'Twopence a week, and jam every other day.'

Alice couldn't help laughing, as she said, 'I don't want you to hire *me* – and I don't care for jam.'

'It's very good jam,' said the Queen.

'Well, I don't want any *today*, at any rate.'

'You couldn't have it if you *did* want it,' the Queen said.

'The rule is, jam tomorrow and jam yesterday – but never jam *today*.'

'It *must* come sometimes to "jam today,"' Alice objected.

'No, it can't,' said the Queen. 'It's jam every *other* day: today isn't any *other* day, you know.'

'I don't understand you,' said Alice. 'It's dreadfully confusing!'

'That's the effect of living backwards,' the Queen said kindly: 'it always makes one a little giddy at first –'

'Living backwards!' Alice repeated in great astonishment. 'I never heard of such a thing!'

'– but there's one great advantage in it, that one's memory works both ways.'

'I'm sure *mine* only works one way,' Alice remarked. 'I can't remember things before they happen.

'It's a poor sort of memory that only works backwards,'

'What sort of thing do *you* remember best?' Alice ventured to ask.

'Oh, things that happened the week after next,' the Queen replied in a careless tone. 'For instance, now,' she went on, sticking a large piece of plaster on her finger as she spoke, 'there's the King's Messenger. He's in prison now, being punished: and the trial doesn't even begin till next Wednesday: and of course the crime comes last of all.'

'Suppose he never commits the crime?' said Alice.

'That would be all the better, wouldn't it?' the Queen said, as she bound the plaster round her finger with a bit of ribbon.

Alice felt there was no denying *that*. 'Of course it would be all the better,' she said: 'but it wouldn't be all the better his being punished.'

'You're wrong *there*, at any rate,' said the Queen. 'Were *you* ever punished?'

'Only for faults,' said Alice.

'And you were all the better for it, I know!' the Queen said triumphantly.

'Yes, but then I *had* done the things I was punished for,' said Alice: 'that makes all the difference.'

'But if you *hadn't* done them,' the Queen said, 'that would have been better still; better, and better, and better!' Her voice went higher with each 'better,' till it got quite to a squeak at last.

Alice was just beginning to say, 'There's a mistake somewhere –,' when the Queen began screaming, so loud that she had to leave the sentence unfinished. 'Oh, oh, oh!' shouted the Queen, shaking her hand about as if she wanted to shake it off. 'My finger's bleeding! Oh, oh, oh, oh!'

Her screams were so exactly like the whistle of a steam engine, that Alice had to hold both her hands over her ears.

'What *is* the matter?' she said, as soon as there was a chance of making herself heard. 'Have you pricked your finger?'

'I haven't pricked it *yet*,' the Queen said, 'but I soon shall – oh, oh, oh!'

'When do you expect to do it?' Alice asked, feeling very much inclined to laugh.

'When I fasten my shawl again,' the poor Queen groaned out: 'the brooch will come undone directly. Oh, oh!' As she said the words the brooch flew open, and the Queen clutched wildly at it, and tried to clasp it again.

'Take care!' cried Alice. 'You're holding it all crooked!' And she caught at the brooch; but it was too late: the pin had slipped, and the Queen had pricked her finger.

'That accounts for the bleeding, you see,' she said to Alice with a smile. 'Now you understand the way things happen here.'

'But why don't you scream *now?*' Alice asked, holding her hands ready to put over her ears again.

'Why, I've done all the screaming already,' said the Queen. 'What would be the good of having it all over again?'

By this time it was getting light. 'The crow must have flown away, I think,' said Alice: 'I'm so glad it's gone. I thought it was the night coming on.'

'I wish *I* could manage to be glad!' the Queen said. 'Only I never can remember the rule. You must be very happy, living in this wood, and being glad whenever you like!'

'Only it is so *very* lonely here!' Alice said in a melancholy voice; and, at the thought of her loneliness, two large tears came rolling down her cheeks.

'Oh, don't go on like that!' cried the poor Queen, wringing her hands in despair. 'Consider what a great girl you are. Consider what a long way you've come today. Consider what o'clock it is. Consider anything, only don't cry!'

Alice could not help laughing at this, even in the midst of her tears. 'Can *you* keep from crying by considering things?' she asked.

'That's the way it's done,' the Queen said with great decision: 'nobody can do two things at once, you know. Let's consider your age to begin with – how old are you?'

'I'm seven and a half, exactly.'

'You needn't say "exactually,"' the Queen remarked. 'I can believe it without that. Now I'll give you something to believe. I'm just one hundred and one, five months and a day.'

'I can't believe *that!*' said Alice.

'Can't you?' the Queen said in a pitying tone. 'Try again: draw a long breath, and shut your eyes.'

Alice laughed. 'There's no use trying,' she said: 'one *can't* believe impossible things.'

'I dare say you haven't had much practice,' said the Queen. 'When I was your age I always did it for half an hour a day. Why, sometimes I've believed as many as six impossible things before breakfast. There goes the shawl again!'

The brooch had come undone as she spoke, and a sudden gust of wind blew the Queen's shawl across a little brook. The Queen spread out her arms again, and went flying after it, and this time she succeeded in catching it for herself. 'I've got it!' she cried in a triumphant tone.

'Now you shall see me pin it on again, all by myself!'

'Then I hope your finger is better now?' Alice said very politely, as she crossed the little brook after the Queen.

'Oh, much better!' cried the Queen, her voice rising into a squeak as she went on. 'Much be-etter! Be-etter! Be-e-e-etter! Be-e-hh!' The last word ended in a long bleat, so like a sheep that Alice quite started.

She looked at the Queen, who seemed to have suddenly wrapped herself up in wool. Alice rubbed her eyes, and looked again. She couldn't make out what had happened at all. Was she in a shop? And was that really – was it really a *sheep* that was sitting on the other side of the counter? Rub as she would, she could make nothing more of it: she was in a little dark shop, leaning with her elbows on the counter, and opposite to her was an old Sheep, sitting in an armchair, knitting, and every now and then leaving off to look at her through a great pair of spectacles.

'What is it you want to buy?' the Sheep said at last, looking up for a moment from her knitting.

'I don't *quite* know yet,' Alice said very gently. 'I should like to look all round me first, if I might.'

'You may look in front of you, and on both sides, if you like,' said the Sheep; 'but you can't look *all* round you – unless you've got eyes at the back of your head.'

But these, as it happened, Alice had *not* got; so she contented herself with turning round, looking at the shelves as she came to them.

The shop seemed to be full of all manner of curious things – but the oddest part of it all was, that whenever she looked hard at any shelf, to make out exactly what it had on it, that particular shelf was always quite empty, though the others round it were crowded as full as they could hold.

'Things flow about so here!' she said at last in a plaintive tone, after she had spent a minute or so in vainly pursuing a large bright thing, that looked sometimes like a doll and sometimes like a work-box, and was always in the shelf next above the one she was looking at. 'And this one is the most provoking of all – but I'll tell you what –' she added, as a sudden thought struck her, 'I'll follow it up to the very top shelf of all. It'll puzzle it to go through the ceiling, I expect!'

But even this plan failed: the 'thing' went through the ceiling as quietly as possible, as if it were quite used to it.

'Are you a child or a teetotum?' the Sheep said, as she took up another pair of needles. 'You'll make me giddy soon, if you go on turning round like that.' She was now working with fourteen pairs at once, and Alice couldn't help looking at her in great astonishment.

'How *can* she knit with so many?' the puzzled child thought to herself. 'She gets more and more like a porcupine every minute!'

'Can you row?' the Sheep asked, handing her a pair of knitting needles as she spoke.

'Yes, a little – but not on land – and not with needles –' Alice was beginning to say, when suddenly the needles turned into oars in her hands, and she found they were in a little boat, gliding along between banks: so there was nothing for it but to do her best.

'Feather!' cried the Sheep, as she took up another pair of needles.

This didn't sound like a remark that needed any answer: so Alice said nothing, but pulled away. There was

something very queer about the water, she thought, as every now and then the oars got fast in it, and would hardly come out again.

'Feather! Feather!' the Sheep cried again, taking more needles. 'You'll be catching a crab directly.'

'A dear little crab!' thought Alice. 'I should like that.'

'Didn't you hear me say "Feather"?' the Sheep cried angrily, taking up quite a bunch of needles.

'Indeed I did,' said Alice: 'you've said it very often – and very loud. Please, where *are* the crabs?'

'In the water, of course!' said the Sheep, sticking

some of the needles into her hair, as her hands were full. 'Feather, I say!'

'*Why* do you say "Feather" so often?' Alice asked at last, rather vexed. 'I'm not a bird!'

'You are,' said the Sheep: 'you're a little goose.'

This offended Alice a little, so there was no more conversation for a minute or two, while the boat glided gently on, sometimes among beds of weeds (which made the oars stick fast in the water, worse than ever), and sometimes under trees, but always with the same tall riverbanks frowning over their heads.

'Oh, please! There are some scented rushes!' Alice cried in a sudden transport of delight. 'There really are – and *such* beauties!'

'You needn't say "please" to *me* about 'em,' the Sheep said, without looking up from her knitting: 'I didn't put 'em there, and I'm not going to take 'em away.'

'No, but I meant – please, may we wait and pick some?' Alice pleaded. 'If you don't mind stopping the boat for a minute.'

'How am *I* to stop it?' said the Sheep. 'If you leave off rowing, it'll stop of itself.'

So the boat was left to drift down the stream as it would, till it glided gently in among the waving rushes. And then the little sleeves were carefully rolled up, and the little arms were plunged in elbow-deep, to get hold of the rushes a good long way down before breaking them off – and for a while Alice forgot all about the Sheep and the knitting, as she bent over the side of the boat, with just the ends of her tangled hair dipping into the water – while with bright eager eyes she caught at one bunch after another of the darling scented rushes.

'I only hope the boat won't tipple over!' she said to

herself. 'Oh, *what* a lovely one! Only I couldn't quite reach it.' And it certainly *did* seem a little provoking ('almost as if it happened on purpose,' she thought) that, though she managed to pick plenty of beautiful rushes as the boat glided by, there was always a more lovely one that she couldn't reach.

'The prettiest are always farther!' she said at last, with a sigh at the obstinacy of the rushes in growing so far off, as, with flushed cheeks and dripping hair and hands, she scrambled back into her place, and began to arrange her new-found treasures.

What mattered it to her just then that the rushes had begun to fade, and to lose all their scent and beauty, from the very moment that she picked them? Even real scented rushes, you know, last only a very little while – and these, being dream-rushes, melted away almost like snow, as they lay in heaps at her feet – but Alice hardly noticed this, there were so many other curious things to think about.

They hadn't gone much farther before the blade of one of the oars got fast in the water and *wouldn't* come out again (so Alice explained it afterwards), and the consequence was that the handle of it caught her under the chin, and, in spite of a series of little shrieks of 'Oh, oh, oh!' from poor Alice, it swept her straight off the seat, and down among the heap of rushes.

However, she wasn't a bit hurt, and was soon up again: the Sheep went on with her knitting all the while, just as if nothing had happened. 'That was a nice crab you caught!' she remarked, as Alice got back into her place, very much relieved to find herself still in the boat.

'Was it? I didn't see it,' said Alice, peeping cautiously over the side of the boat into the dark water. 'I wish it hadn't let go – I should so like a little crab to take home with me!' But the Sheep only laughed scornfully, and went on with her knitting.

'Are there many crabs there?' said Alice.

'Crabs and all sorts of things,' said the Sheep: 'plenty of choice, only make up your mind. Now, what *do* you want to buy?'

'To buy!' Alice echoed in a tone that was half astonished and half frightened – for the oars, and the boat, and the river, had vanished all in a moment, and she was back again in the little dark shop.

'I should like to buy an egg, please,' she said timidly. 'How do you sell them?'

'Fivepence farthing for one – twopence for two,' the Sheep replied.

'Then two are cheaper than one!' Alice said in a surprised tone, taking out her purse.

'Only you *must* eat them both, if you buy two,' said the Sheep.

'Then I'll have *one*, please,' said Alice, as she put the money down on the counter. For she thought to herself, 'They mightn't be at all nice, you know.'

The Sheep took the money and put it away in a box: then she said, 'I never put things into people's hands – that would never do – you must get it for yourself.' And so saying, she went off to the other end of the shop, and set the egg upright on a shelf.

'I wonder *why* it wouldn't do?' thought Alice, as she groped her way among the tables and chairs, for the shop was very dark towards the end. 'The egg seems to get farther away the more I walk towards it. Let me see, is this a chair? Why, it's got branches, I declare! How very odd to find trees growing here! And actually here's a little brook! Well, this is the very queerest shop I ever saw!'

So she went on, wondering more and more at every step, as everything turned into a tree the moment she came up to it, and she quite expected the egg to do the same.

CHAPTER 6

Humpty Dumpty

However, the egg only got larger and larger, and more and more human: when she had come within a few yards of it, she saw that it had eyes and a nose and mouth; and when she had come close to it, she saw clearly that it was HUMPTY DUMPTY himself. 'It can't be anybody else!' she said to herself. 'I'm as certain of it, as if his name were written all over his face!'

It might have been written a hundred times, easily, on that enormous face. Humpty Dumpty was sitting with his legs crossed, like a Turk, on the top of a high wall – such a narrow one that Alice quite wondered how he could keep his balance – and, as his eyes were steadily fixed in the opposite direction, and he didn't take the least notice of her, she thought he must be a stuffed figure after all.

'And how exactly like an egg he is!' she said aloud, standing with her hands ready to catch him, for she was every moment expecting him to fall.

'It's *very* provoking,' Humpty Dumpty said, after a long silence, looking away from Alice as he spoke, 'to be called an egg – *very!*'

'I said you *looked* like an egg, Sir,' Alice gently explained. 'And some eggs are very pretty, you know,' she added, hoping to turn her remark into a sort of compliment.

'Some people,' said Humpty Dumpty, looking away from her as usual, 'have no more sense than a baby!'

Alice didn't know what to say to this: it wasn't at all like conversation, she thought, as he never said anything to *her*; in fact, his last remark was evidently addressed to a tree – so she stood and softly repeated to herself:

> *Humpty Dumpty sat on a wall:*
> *Humpty Dumpty had a great fall.*
> *All the King's horses and all the King's men*
> *Couldn't put Humpty Dumpty in his place again.'*

'That last line is much too long for the poetry,' she added almost out loud, forgetting that Humpty Dumpty would hear her.

'Don't stand chattering to yourself like that,' Humpty Dumpty said, looking at her for the first time, 'but tell me your name and your business.'

'My *name* is Alice, but –'

'It's a stupid name enough!' Humpty Dumpty interrupted impatiently. 'What does it mean?'

'*Must* a name mean something?' Alice asked doubtfully.

'Of course it must,' Humpty Dumpty said with a short laugh: '*my* name means the shape I am – and a good handsome shape it is, too. With a name like yours, you might be any shape, almost.'

'Why do you sit out here all alone?' said Alice,

not wishing to begin an argument.

'Why, because there's nobody with me!' cried Humpty Dumpty. 'Did you think I didn't know the answer to *that?* Ask another.'

'Don't you think you'd be safer down on the ground?' Alice went on, not with any idea of making another riddle, but simply in her good-natured anxiety for the queer creature. 'That wall is so *very* narrow!'

'What tremendously easy riddles you ask!' Humpty Dumpty growled out. 'Of course I don't think so! Why, if ever I *did* fall off – which there's no chance of – but *if* I did –' Here he pursed up his lips, and looked so solemn and grand that Alice could hardly help laughing. '*If* I *did* fall,' he went on, '*the King has promised me –* ah, you may turn pale, if you like! You didn't think I was going to say that, did you? *The King has promised me – with his very own mouth – to – to –*'

'To send all his horses and all his men,' Alice interrupted, rather unwisely.

'Now I declare that's too bad!' Humpty Dumpty cried, breaking into a sudden passion. 'You've been listening at doors – and behind trees – and down chimneys – or you couldn't have known it!'

'I haven't, indeed!' Alice said very gently. 'It's in a book.'

'Ah, well! They may write such things in a *book*,' Humpty Dumpty said in a calmer tone. 'That's what you call a History of England, that is. Now, take a good look at me! I'm one that has spoken to a King, *I* am: mayhap you'll never see such another: and to show you I'm not proud, you may shake hands with me!' And he grinned almost from ear to ear, as he leant forwards (and as nearly as possible fell off the wall in doing so) and offered Alice his hand. She watched him a little anxiously as she took it. 'If he smiled much more, the ends of his mouth might meet behind,' she thought: 'and then I don't know *what* would happen to his head! I'm afraid it would come off!'

'Yes, all his horses and all his men,' Humpty Dumpty went on. 'They'd pick me up again in a minute, *they* would! However, this conversation is going on a little too fast: let's go back to the last remark but one.'

'I'm afraid I can't quite remember it,' Alice said very politely.

'In that case we may start afresh,' said Humpty Dumpty, 'and it's my turn to choose a subject –' ('He talks about it just as if it was a game!' thought Alice.) 'So here's a question for you. How old did you say you were?'

Alice made a short calculation, and said, 'Seven years and six months.'

'Wrong!' Humpty Dumpty exclaimed triumphantly. 'You never said a word like it.'

'I thought you meant "How old *are* you?"' Alice explained.

'If I'd meant that, I'd have said it,' said Humpty Dumpty.

Alice didn't want to begin another argument, so she said nothing.

'Seven years and six months!' Humpty Dumpty repeated thoughtfully. 'An uncomfortable sort of age. Now if you'd asked *my* advice, I'd have said, "Leave off at seven" – but it's too late now.'

'I never ask advice about growing,' Alice said indignantly.

'Too proud?' the other inquired.

Alice felt even more indignant at this suggestion. 'I mean,' she said, 'that one can't help growing older.'

'*One* can't, perhaps,' said Humpty Dumpty, 'but *two* can. With proper assistance, you might have left off at seven.'

'What a beautiful belt you've got on!' Alice suddenly remarked. (They had had quite enough of the subject of age, she thought: and if they really were to take turns in choosing subjects, it was *her* turn now.) 'At least,' she corrected herself on second thoughts, 'a beautiful cravat, I should have said – no, a belt, I mean – I beg your pardon!' she added in dismay, for Humpty Dumpty looked thoroughly offended, and she began to wish she hadn't chosen that subject. 'If only I knew,' she thought to herself, 'which was neck and which was waist!'

Evidently Humpty Dumpty was very angry, though he said nothing for a minute or two. When he *did* speak again, it was in a deep growl.

'It is a – *most* – *provoking* – thing,' he said at last, 'when a person doesn't know a cravat from a belt!'

'I know it's very ignorant of me,' Alice said in so humble a tone that Humpty Dumpty relented.

'It's a cravat, child, and a beautiful one, as you say. It's a present from the White King and Queen. There now!'

'Is it really?' said Alice, quite pleased to find she *had* chosen a good subject after all.

'They gave it me,' Humpty Dumpty continued thoughtfully, as he crossed one knee over the other and clasped his hands round it, 'they gave it me – for an un-birthday present.'

'I beg your pardon?' Alice said, with a puzzled air.

'I'm not offended,' said Humpty Dumpty.

'I mean what *is* an un-birthday present?'

'A present given when it isn't your birthday, of course.'

Alice considered a little. 'I like birthday presents best,' she said at last.

'You don't know what you're talking about!' cried Humpty Dumpty. 'How many days are there in a year?'

'Three hundred and sixty-five,' said Alice

'And how many birthdays have you?'

'One.'

'And if you take one from three hundred and sixty-five, what remains?'

'Three hundred and sixty-four, of course.'

Humpty Dumpty looked doubtful. 'I'd rather see that done on paper,' he said.

Alice couldn't help smiling as she took out her memorandum-book, and worked the sum for him:

$$
\begin{array}{r}
365 \\
1 \\
\hline
364 \\
\hline
\end{array}
$$

Humpty Dumpty took the book, and looked at it carefully. 'That seems to be done right –' he began.

'You're holding it upside down!' Alice interrupted.

'To be sure I was!' Humpty Dumpty said gaily, as she turned it round for him. 'I thought it looked a little queer. As I was saying, that *seems* to be done right – though I haven't time to look it over thoroughly just now – and that shows that there are three hundred and sixty-four days when you might get un-birthday presents –'

'Certainly,' said Alice.

'And only *one* for birthday presents, you know. There's glory for you!'

'I don't know what you mean by "glory,"' Alice said.

Humpty Dumpty smiled contemptuously. 'Of course you don't – till I tell you. I meant "there's a nice knock-down argument for you!"'

'But "glory" doesn't mean "a nice knockdown-argument,"' Alice objected.

'When I use a word,' Humpty Dumpty said in rather a scornful tone, 'it means just what I choose it to mean – neither more nor less.'

'The question is,' said Alice, 'whether you *can* make words mean so many different things.'

'The question is,' said Humpty Dumpty, 'which is to be Master – that's all.'

Alice was too much puzzled to say anything, so after a minute Humpty Dumpty began again. 'They've a temper, some of them – particularly verbs, they're the proudest – adjectives you can do anything with, but not verbs – however, *I* can manage the whole lot of them! Impenetrability! That's what *I* say!'

'Would you tell me, please,' said Alice, 'what that means?'

'Now you talk like a reasonable child,' said Humpty Dumpty, looking very much pleased. 'I meant by "impenetrability" that we've had enough of that subject, and it would be just as well if you'd mention what you mean to do next, as I suppose you don't mean to stop here all the rest of your life.'

'That's a great deal to make one word mean,' Alice said in a thoughtful tone.

'When I make a word to do a lot of work like that,' said Humpty Dumpty, 'I always pay it extra.'

'Oh!' said Alice. She was too much puzzled to make any other remark.

'Ah, you should see 'em come round me of a Saturday night,' Humpty Dumpty went on, wagging his head gravely from side to side: 'for to get their wages, you know.'

(Alice didn't venture to ask what he paid them with; and so you see I can't tell *you*.)

'You seem very clever at explaining words, Sir,' said Alice. 'Would you kindly tell me the meaning of the poem called "Jabberwocky"?'

'Let's hear it,' said Humpty Dumpty. 'I can explain

all the poems that ever were invented – and a good many that haven't been invented just yet.'

This sounded very hopeful, so Alice repeated the first verse:

> *'Twas brillig, and the slithy toves*
> *Did gyre and gimble in the wabe:*
> *All mimsy were the borogoves,*
> *And the mome raths outgrabe.'*

'That's enough to begin with,' Humpty Dumpty interrupted: 'there are plenty of hard words there. "*Brillig*" means four o'clock in the afternoon – the time when you begin *broiling* things for dinner.'

'That'll do very well,' said Alice: 'and "*slithy*"?'

'Well, "*slithy*" means "lithe and slimy." "Lithe" is the same as "active." You see it's like a portmanteau – there are two meanings packed up into one word.'

'I see it now,' Alice remarked thoughtfully: 'and what are "*toves*"?'

'Well, "*toves*" are something like badgers – they're something like lizards – and they're something like corkscrews.'

'They must be very curious-looking creatures.'

'They are that,' said Humpty Dumpty: 'also they make their nests under sundials – also they live on cheese.'

'And what's to "*gyre*" and to "*gimble*"?'

'To "*gyre*" is to go round and round like a gyroscope. To "*gimble*" is to make holes like a gimlet.'

'And "*the wabe*,' is the grass-plot round a sundial, I suppose?' said Alice, surprised at her own ingenuity.

'Of course it is. It's called "*wabe*," you know,

because it goes a long way before it, and a long way behind it –'

'And a long way beyond it on each side,' Alice added.

'Exactly so. Well then "*mimsy*" is "flimsy and miserable" (there's another portmanteau for you). And a "*borogove*" is a thin shabby-looking bird with its feathers sticking out all round – something like a live mop.'

'And then "*mome raths*"?' said Alice. 'I'm afraid I'm giving you a great deal of trouble.'

'Well, a "*rath*" is a sort of green pig: but "*mome*" I'm not certain about. I think it's short "from home" – meaning that they'd lost their way, you know.'

'And what does "*outgrabe*" mean?'

'Well, "*outgribing*" is something between bellowing and whistling, with a kind of sneeze in the middle: however, you'll hear it done, maybe – down in the wood yonder – and when you've once heard it you'll be *quite* content. Who's been repeating all that hard stuff to you?'

'I read it in a book,' said Alice. 'But I *had* some poetry repeated to me, much easier than that, by – Tweedledee, I think.'

'As to poetry, you know,' said Humpty Dumpty, stretching out one of his great hands, '*I* can repeat poetry as well as other folk, if it comes to that –'

'Oh, it needn't come to that!' Alice hastily said, hoping to keep him from beginning.

'The piece I'm going to repeat,' he went on, without noticing her remark, 'was written entirely for your amusement.'

Alice felt that in that case she really *ought* to listen to it, so she sat down, and said, 'Thank you' rather sadly.

> '*In winter, when the fields are white,*
> *I sing this song for your delight –*

only I don't sing it,' he added, as an explanation.

'I see you don't,' said Alice.

'If you can *see* whether I'm singing or not, you've sharper eyes than most,' Humpty Dumpty remarked severely. Alice was silent.

> '*In spring, when woods are getting green,*
> *I'll try and tell you what I mean.*'

'Thank you very much,' said Alice

> *'In summer, when the days are long,*
> *Perhaps you'll understand the song:*
>
> *In autumn, when the leaves are brown,*
> *Take pen and ink, and write it down.'*

'I will if I can remember it so long,' said Alice.

'You needn't go on making remarks like that,' Humpty Dumpty said: 'they're not sensible, and they put me out.'

> *'I sent a message to the fish:*
> *I told them "This is what I wish."*
>
> *The little fishes of the sea*
> *They sent an answer back to me.*
>
> *The little fishes' answer was*
> *"We cannot do it, Sir, because —"'*

'I'm afraid I don't quite understand,' said Alice. 'It gets easier farther on,' Humpty Dumpty replied.

> *'I sent to them again to say*
> *"It will be better to obey."*
>
> *The fishes answered with a grin,*
> *"Why, what a temper you are in!"*
>
> *I told them once, I told them twice:*
> *They would not listen to advice.*

I took a kettle large and new,
Fit for the deed I had to do.

My heart went hop, my heart went thump;
I filled the kettle at the pump.

Then some one came to me and said,
"The little fishes are in bed."

I said to him, I said it plain,
"Then you must wake them up again."

I said it very loud and clear;
I went and shouted in his ear."

Humpty Dumpty raised his voice almost to a scream as he repeated this verse, and Alice thought with a shudder, 'I wouldn't have been the messenger for *anything!*'

'But he was very stiff and proud;
He said, "You needn't shout so loud!"

And he was very proud and stiff;
He said, "I'd go and wake them, if –"

I took a corkscrew from the shelf:
I went to wake them up myself.

And when I found the door was locked,
I pulled and pushed and kicked and
knocked.

> *And when I found the door was shut,*
> *I tried to turn the handle, but –'*

There was a long pause.

'Is that all?' Alice timidly asked.

'That's all,' said Humpty Dumpty. 'Goodbye.'

This was rather sudden, Alice thought: but, after such a *very* strong hint that she ought to be going, she felt that it would hardly be civil to stay. So she got up, and held out her hand. 'Goodbye, till we meet again!' she said as cheerfully as she could.

'I shouldn't know you again if we *did* meet,' Humpty Dumpty replied in a discontented tone, giving her one of his fingers to shake; 'you're so exactly like other people.'

'The face is what one goes by, generally,' Alice remarked in a thoughtful tone.

'That's just what I complain of,' said Humpty Dumpty. 'Your face is the same as everybody has – the two eyes, so –' (marking their places in the air with his thumb), 'nose in the middle, mouth under. It's always the same. Now if you had the two eyes on the same side of the nose, for instance – or the mouth at the top – that would be *some* help.'

'It wouldn't look nice,' Alice objected. But Humpty Dumpty only shut his eyes and said, 'Wait till you've tried.'

Alice waited a minute to see if he would speak again, but as he never opened his eyes or took any further notice of her, she said 'Goodbye!' once more, and getting no answer to this, she quietly walked away: but she couldn't help saying to herself as she went, 'Of all the unsatis-factory –' (she repeated this aloud, as it was a great

comfort to have such a long word to say) 'of all the un-satisfactory people I *ever* met –' She never finished the sentence, for at this moment a heavy crash shook the forest from end to end.

CHAPTER 7

The Lion and the Unicorn

The next moment soldiers came running through the wood, at first in twos and threes, then ten or twenty together, and at last in such crowds that they seemed to fill the whole forest. Alice got behind a tree, for fear of being run over, and watched them go by.

She thought that in all her life she had never seen soldiers so uncertain on their feet: they were always tripping over something or other, and whenever one went down, several more always fell over him, so that the ground was soon covered with little heaps of men.

Then came the horses. Having four feet, these managed rather better than the foot-soldiers: but even *they* stumbled now and then; and it seemed to be a regular rule that, whenever a horse stumbled, the rider fell off instantly. The confusion got worse every moment, and Alice was very glad to get out of the wood into an open place, where she found the White King seated on the ground, busily writing in his memorandum-book.

'I've sent them all!' the King cried in a tone of

delight, on seeing Alice. 'Did you happen to meet any soldiers, my dear, as you came through the wood?'

'Yes, I did,' said Alice: 'several thousand, I should think.'

'Four thousand two hundred and seven, that's the exact number,' the King said, referring to his book. 'I couldn't send all the horses, you know, because two of them are wanted in the game. And I haven't sent the two messengers, either. They're both gone to the town. Just look along the road and tell me if you can see either of them.'

'I see nobody on the road,' said Alice.

'I only wish *I* had such eyes,' the King remarked in a fretful tone. 'To be able to see Nobody! And at that distance too! Why, it's as much as I can do to see real people, by this light!'

All this was lost on Alice, who was still looking intently along the road, shading her eyes with one hand. 'I see somebody now!' she exclaimed at last. 'But he's coming very slowly – and what curious attitudes he goes into!' (For the Messenger kept skipping up and down, and wriggling like an eel, as he came along, with his great hands spread out like fans on each side.)

'Not at all,' said the King. 'He's an Anglo-Saxon Messenger – and those are Anglo-Saxon attitudes. He only does them when he's happy. His name is Haigha.' (He pronounced it so as to rhyme with 'mayor.')

'I love my love with an H,' Alice couldn't help beginning, 'because he is Happy. I hate him with an H, because he is Hideous. I fed him with – with – with Ham-sandwiches and Hay. His name is Haigha, and he lives –'

'He lives on the Hill,' the King remarked simply, without the least idea that he was joining in the game, while Alice was still hesitating for the name of a town beginning with H. 'The other Messenger's called Hatta. I must have *two*, you know – to come and go. One to come, and one to go.'

'I beg your pardon?' said Alice.

'It isn't respectable to beg,' said the King.

'I only meant that I didn't understand,' said Alice. 'Why one to come and one to go?'

'Don't I tell you?' the King repeated impatiently. 'I must have *two* – to fetch and carry. One to fetch, and one to carry.'

At this moment the Messenger arrived: he was far

too much out of breath to say a word, and could only wave his hands about, and make the most fearful faces at the poor King.

'This young lady loves you with an H,' the King said, introducing Alice in the hope of turning off the Messenger's attention from himself – but it was of no use – the Anglo-Saxon attitudes only got more extraordinary every moment, while the great eyes rolled wildly from side to side.

'You alarm me!' said the King. 'I feel faint – Give me a ham sandwich!'

On which the Messenger, to Alice's great amusement, opened a bag that hung round his neck, and handed a sandwich to the King, who devoured it greedily.

'Another sandwich!' said the King.

'There's nothing but hay left now,' the Messenger said, peeping into the bag.

'Hay, then,' the King murmured in a faint whisper.

Alice was glad to see that it revived him a good deal.

'There's nothing like eating hay when you're faint,' he remarked to her, as he munched away.

'I should think throwing cold water over you would be better,' Alice suggested: '– or some sal-volatile.'

'I didn't say there was nothing *better*,' the King replied. 'I said there was nothing *like* it.' Which Alice did not venture to deny.

'Who did you pass on the road?' the King went on, holding out his hand to the Messenger for some more hay.

'Nobody,' said the Messenger.

'Quite right,' said the King: 'this young lady saw him too. So of course Nobody walks slower than you.'

'I do my best,' the Messenger said in a sullen tone. 'I'm sure nobody walks much faster than I do!'

'He can't do that,' said the King, 'or else he'd have been here first. However, now you've got your breath, you may tell us what's happened in the town.'

'I'll whisper it,' said the Messenger, putting his hands to his mouth in the shape of a trumpet, and stooping so as to get close to the King's ear. Alice was sorry for this, as she wanted to hear the news too. However, instead of whispering, he simply shouted at the top of his voice, 'They're at it again!'

'Do you call *that* a whisper!' cried the poor King, jumping up and shaking himself. 'If you do such a thing again I'll have you buttered! It went through and through my head like an earthquake!'

'It would have to be a very tiny earthquake!' thought Alice. 'Who are at it again?' she ventured to ask.

'Why, the Lion and the Unicorn, of course,' said the King.

'Fighting for the crown?'

'Yes, to be sure,' said the King: 'and the best of the joke is, that it's *my* crown all the while! Let's run and see them.' And they trotted off, Alice repeating to herself, as she ran, the words of the old song: –

> *'The Lion and the Unicorn were fighting for the crown:*
> *The Lion beat the Unicorn all round the town.*
> *Some gave them white bread, some gave them brown:*
> *Some gave them plum-cake and drummed them out*
> *of town.'*

'Does – the one – that wins – get the crown?' she asked, as well as she could, for the run was putting her quite out of breath.

'Dear me, no!' said the King. 'What an idea!'

'Would you – be good enough –' Alice panted out, after running a little farther, 'to stop a minute – just to get – one's breath again?'

'I'm *good* enough, the King said, 'only I'm not *strong* enough. You see, a minute goes by so fearfully quick. You might as well try to stop a Bandersnatch!'

Alice had no more breath for talking, so they trotted on in silence, till they came in sight of a great crowd, in the middle of which the Lion and Unicorn were fighting. They were in such a cloud of dust, that at first Alice could not make out which was which: but she soon managed to distinguish the Unicorn by his horn.

They placed themselves close to where Hatta, the other Messenger, was standing watching the fight, with a cup of tea in one hand and a piece of bread-and-butter in the other.

'He's only just out of prison, and he hadn't finished his tea when he was sent in,' Haigha whispered to Alice:

'and they only give them oyster shells in there – so you see he's very hungry and thirsty. How are you, dear child?' he went on, putting his arm affectionately round Hatta's neck.

Hatta looked round and nodded, and went on with his bread-and-butter.

'Were you happy in prison, dear child?' said Haigha.

Hatta looked round once more, and this time a tear or two trickled down his cheek: but not a word would he say.

'Speak, can't you!' Haigha cried impatiently. But Hatta only munched away, and drank some more tea.

'Speak, won't you!' cried the King. 'How are they getting on with the fight?'

Hatta made a desperate effort, and swallowed a large piece of bread-and-butter. 'They're getting on very well,' he said in a choking voice: 'each of them has been down about eighty-seven times.'

'Then I suppose they'll soon bring the white bread and the brown?' Alice ventured to remark.

'It's waiting for 'em now,' said Hatta: 'this is a bit of it as I'm eating.'

There was a pause in the fight just then, and the Lion and the Unicorn sat down, panting, while the King called out, 'Ten minutes allowed for refreshments!' Haigha and Hatta set to work at once, carrying round trays of white and brown bread. Alice took a piece to taste, but it was *very* dry.

'I don't think they'll fight any more today,' the King said to Hatta: 'go and order the drums to begin.' And Hatta went bounding away like a grasshopper.

For a minute or two Alice stood silent, watching him. Suddenly she brightened up. 'Look, look!' she cried, pointing eagerly. 'There's the White Queen running across the country! She came flying out of the wood over yonder – How fast those Queens *can* run!'

'There's some enemy after her, no doubt,' the King said, without even looking round. 'That wood's full of them.'

'But aren't you going to run and help her?' Alice asked, very much surprised at his taking it so quietly.

'No use, no use!' said the King. 'She runs so fearfully quick. You might as well try to catch a Bandersnatch! But I'll make a memorandum about her, if you like – She's a dear good creature,' he repeated softly to himself, as he opened his memorandum-book. 'Do you spell "creature" with a double "e"?'

At this moment the Unicorn sauntered by them, with his hands in his pockets. 'I had the best of it this time!' he said to the King, just glancing at him as he passed.

'A little – a little,' the King replied, rather nervously.

LEWIS CARROLL

'You shouldn't have run him through with your horn, you know.'

'It didn't hurt him,' the Unicorn said carelessly, and he was going on, when his eye happened to fall upon Alice: he turned round instantly, and stood for some time looking at her with an air of the deepest disgust.

'What – is – this?' he said at last.

'This is a child!' Haigha replied eagerly, coming in front of Alice to introduce her, and spreading out both his hands towards her in an Anglo-Saxon attitude. 'We only found it today. It's as large as life, and twice as natural!'

'I always thought they were fabulous monsters!' said the Unicorn. 'Is it alive?'

'It can talk,' said Haigha solemnly.

The Unicorn looked dreamily at Alice, and said, 'Talk, child.'

Alice could not help her lips curling up into a smile as she began: 'Do you know, I always thought Unicorns were fabulous monsters, too! I never saw one alive before!'

'Well, now that we *have* seen each other,' said the Unicorn, 'if you'll believe in me, I'll believe in you. Is that a bargain?'

'Yes, if you like,' said Alice.

'Come, fetch out the plum-cake, old man!' the Unicorn went on, turning from her to the King. 'None of your brown bread for me!'

'Certainly – certainly!' the King muttered, and beckoned to Haigha. 'Open the bag!' he whispered. 'Quick! Not that one – that's full of hay!'

Haigha took a large cake out of the bag, and gave it to Alice to hold, while he got out a dish and carving-knife.

How they all came out of it Alice couldn't guess. It was just like a conjuring trick, she thought.

The Lion had joined them while this was going on: he looked very tired and sleepy, and his eyes were half shut. 'What's this?' he said, blinking lazily at Alice, and speaking in a deep hollow tone that sounded like the tolling of a great bell.

'Ah, what *is* it, now?' the Unicorn cried eagerly. 'You'll never guess! *I* couldn't.'

The Lion looked at Alice wearily. 'Are you animal – or vegetable – or mineral?' he said, yawning at every other word.

'It's a fabulous monster!' the Unicorn cried out before Alice could reply.

'Then hand round the plum-cake, Monster,' the Lion said, lying down and putting his chin on his paws. 'And sit down, both of you' (to the King and the Unicorn): 'fair play with the cake, you know!'

The King was evidently very uncomfortable at

having to sit down between the two great creatures: but there was no other place for him.

'What a fight we might have for the crown, *now!*' the Unicorn said, looking slyly up at the crown, which the poor King was nearly shaking off his head, he trembled so much.

'I should win easy,' said the Lion.

'I'm not so sure of that,' said the Unicorn.

'Why, I beat you all round the town, you chicken!' the Lion replied angrily, half getting up as he spoke.

Here the King interrupted, to prevent the quarrel going on: he was very nervous, and his voice quite quivered. 'All round the town?' he said. 'That's a good long way. Did you go by the old bridge, or the market place? You get the best view by the old bridge.'

'I'm sure I don't know,' the Lion growled out as he lay down again. 'There was too much dust to see anything. What a time the Monster is cutting up that cake!'

Alice had seated herself on the bank of a little brook, with the great dish on her knees, and was sawing away diligently with the knife. 'It's very provoking!' she said, in reply to the Lion (she was getting quite used to being called "the Monster"). 'I've cut several slices already, but they always join on again!'

'You don't know how to manage Looking-Glass cakes.' the Unicorn remarked. 'Hand it round first, and cut it afterwards.'

This sounded nonsense, but Alice very obediently got up, and carried the dish round, and the cake divided itself into three pieces as she did so. '*Now* cut it up,' said the Lion, as she returned to her place with the empty dish.

'I say, this isn't fair!' cried the Unicorn, as Alice sat with the knife in her hand, very much puzzled how to begin. 'The Monster has given the Lion twice as much as me!'

'She's kept none for herself, anyhow,' said the Lion. 'Do you like plum-cake, Monster?'

But before Alice could answer him, the drums began.

Where the noise came from, she couldn't make out: the air seemed full of it, and it rang through and through her head till she felt quite deafened. She started to her feet and sprang across the little brook in her terror, and had just time to see the Lion and the Unicorn rise to their feet, with angry looks at being interrupted in their feast, before she dropped to her knees, and put her hands

over her ears, vainly trying to shut out the dreadful
uproar.

'If *that* doesn't "drum them out of town,"' she
thought to herself, 'nothing ever will!'

CHAPTER 8

'It's My Own Invention'

After a while the noise seemed gradually to die away, till all was dead silence, and Alice lifted up her head in some alarm. There was no one to be seen, and her first thought was that she must have been dreaming about the Lion and the Unicorn and those queer Anglo-Saxon Messengers. However, there was the great dish still lying at her feet, on which she had tried to cut the plum-cake, 'So I wasn't dreaming, after all,' she said to herself, 'unless – unless we're all part of the same dream. Only I do hope it's *my* dream, and not the Red King's! I don't like belonging to another person's dream,' she went on in a rather complaining tone: 'I've a great mind to go and wake him, and see what happens!'

At this moment her thoughts were interrupted by a loud shouting of 'Ahoy! Ahoy! Check!' and a Knight, dressed in crimson armour, came galloping down upon her, brandishing a great club. Just as he reached her, the horse stopped suddenly: 'You're my prisoner!' the Knight cried, as he tumbled off his horse.

Startled as she was, Alice was more frightened for

him than for herself at the moment, and watched him with some anxiety as he mounted again. As soon as he was comfortably in the saddle, he began once more. 'You're my –' but here another voice broke in 'Ahoy! Ahoy! Check!' and Alice looked round in some surprise for the new enemy.

This time it was a White Knight. He drew up at Alice's side, and tumbled off his horse just as the Red Knight had done: then he got on again, and the two Knights sat and looked at each other for some time without speaking. Alice looked from one to the other in some bewilderment.

'She's *my* prisoner, you know!' the Red Knight said at last.

'Yes, but then *I* came and rescued her!' the White Knight replied.

'Well, we must fight for her, then,' said the Red Knight as he took up his helmet (which hung from the saddle, and was something the shape of a horse's head), and put it on.

'You will observe the Rules of Battle, of course?' the White Knight remarked, putting on his helmet too.

'I always do,' said the Red Knight, and they began banging away at each other with such fury that Alice got behind a tree to be out of the way of the blows.

'I wonder, now, what the Rules of Battle are,' she said to herself, as she watched the fight, timidly peeping out from her hiding-place: 'one Rule seems to be that, if one Knight hits the other, he knocks him off his horse, and if he misses, he tumbles off himself – and another Rule seems to be that they hold their clubs with their arms, as if they were Punch and Judy. What a noise they make when they tumble! Just like a whole set of fire-irons falling into the fender! And how quiet the horses are! They let them get on and off them just as if they were tables!'

Another Rule of Battle, that Alice had not noticed, seemed to be that they always fell on their heads, and the battle ended with their both falling off in this way, side by side: when they got up again, they shook hands, and then the Red Knight mounted and galloped off.

'It was a glorious victory, wasn't it?' said the White Knight, as he came up panting.

'I don't know,' Alice said doubtfully. 'I don't want to be anybody's prisoner. I want to be a Queen.'

'So you will, when you've crossed the next brook,' said the White Knight. 'I'll see you safe to the end of the wood – and then I must go back, you know. That's the end of my move.'

'Thank you very much,' said Alice. 'May I help you off with your helmet?' It was evidently more than he could manage by himself: however, she managed to shake him out of it at last.

'Now one can breathe more easily,' said the Knight, putting back his shaggy hair with both hands, and turning his gentle face and large mild eyes to Alice. She thought she had never seen such a strange-looking soldier in all her life.

He was dressed in tin armour, which seemed to fit him very badly, and he had a queer-shaped little deal box fastened across his shoulders upside-down, and with the lid hanging open. Alice looked at it with great curiosity.

'I see you're admiring my little box,' the Knight said in a friendly tone. 'It's my own invention – to keep clothes and sandwiches in. You see I carry it upside-down, so that the rain can't get in.'

'But the things can get *out*,' Alice gently remarked. 'Do you know the lid's open?'

'I didn't know it,' the Knight said, a shade of vexation passing over his face. 'Then all the things must have fallen out! And the box is no use without them.' He unfastened it as he spoke, and was just going to throw it into the bushes, when a sudden thought seemed to strike him, and he hung it carefully on a tree. 'Can you guess why I did that?' he said to Alice.

Alice shook her head.

'In hopes some bees may make a nest in it – then I should get the honey.'

'But you've got a bee-hive – or something like one – fastened to the saddle,' said Alice.

Yes, it's a very good bee-hive,' the Knight said in a discontented tone, 'one of the best kind. But not a single bee has come near it yet. And the other thing is a mouse-trap. I suppose the mice keep the bees out – or the bees keep the mice out, I don't know which.'

'I was wondering what the mouse-trap was for,' said Alice. 'It isn't very likely there would be any mice on the horse's back.'

'Not very likely, perhaps,' said the Knight; 'but, if they *do* come, I don't choose to have them running all about.

'You see,' he went on, after a pause, 'it's as well to be provided for *everything.* That's the reason the horse has all these anklets round his feet.'

'But what are they for?' Alice asked in a tone of great curiosity.

'To guard against the bites of sharks,' the Knight replied. 'It's an invention of my own. And now, help me on. I'll go with you to the end of the wood – What's that dish for?'

'It's meant for plum-cake,' said Alice.

'We'd better take it with us,' the Knight said. 'It'll come in handy if we find any plum-cake. Help me to get it into this bag.'

This took a long time to manage, though Alice held the bag open very carefully, because the Knight was so *very* awkward in putting in the dish: the first two or three times that he tried he fell in himself instead. 'It's rather a tight fit, you see,' he said, as they got it in at last; 'there are so many candlesticks in the bag.' And he hung it to the saddle, which was already loaded with bunches of carrots, and fire-irons, and many other things.

'I hope you've got your hair well fastened on?' he continued, as they set off.

'Only in the usual way,' Alice said, smiling.

'That's hardly enough,' he said anxiously.

'You see the wind is so *very* strong here. It's as strong as soup.'

'Have you invented a plan for keeping the hair from being blown off?' Alice inquired.

'Not yet,' said the Knight. 'But I've got a plan for keeping it from *falling* off.'

'I should like to hear it very much.'

'First you take an upright stick,' said the Knight. 'Then you make your hair creep up it, like a fruit tree. Now the reason hair falls off is because it hangs *down* – things never

fall *up*wards, you know. It's a plan of my own invention.
You may try it if you like.'

It didn't sound a comfortable plan, Alice thought,
and for a few minutes she walked on in silence,
puzzling over the idea, and every now and then stopping to help the poor Knight, who certainly was *not* a
good rider.

Whenever the horse stopped (which it did very
often), he fell off in front; and, whenever it went on again
(which it generally did rather suddenly), he fell off
behind. Otherwise he kept on pretty well, except that
he had a habit of now and then falling off sideways; and
as he generally did this on the side on which Alice was
walking, she soon found that it was the best plan not to
walk *quite* close to the horse.

'I'm afraid you've not had much practice in riding,'
she ventured to say, as she was helping him up from his
fifth tumble.

The Knight looked very much surprised, and a little
offended at the remark. 'What makes you say that?' he
asked, as he scrambled back into the saddle, keeping hold
of Alice's hair with one hand, to save himself from falling
over on the other side.

'Because people don't fall off quite so often, when
they've had much practice.'

'I've had plenty of practice,' the Knight said very
gravely: 'plenty of practice!'

Alice could think of nothing better to say than
'Indeed?' but she said it as heartily as she could. They
went on a little way in silence after this, the Knight with
his eyes shut, muttering to himself, and Alice watching
anxiously for the next tumble.

The great art of riding,' the Knight suddenly began

in a loud voice, waving his right arm as he spoke, 'is to keep –'

Here the sentence ended as suddenly as it had begun, as the Knight fell heavily on the top of his head exactly in the path where Alice was walking. She was quite frightened this time, and said in an anxious tone, as she picked him up, 'I hope no bones are broken?'

'None to speak of,' the Knight said, as if he didn't mind breaking two or three of them. 'The great art of riding, as I was saying, is – to keep your balance properly. Like this, you know –'

He let go the bridle, and stretched out both his arms to show Alice what he meant, and this time he fell flat on his back, right under the horse's feet.

'Plenty of practice!' he went on repeating, all the time that Alice was getting him on his feet again. 'Plenty of practice!'

'It's too ridiculous!' cried Alice, losing all her patience this time. 'You ought to have a wooden horse on wheels, that you ought!'

'Does that kind go smoothly!' the Knight asked in a tone of great interest, clasping his arms round the horse's neck as he spoke, just in time to save himself from tumbling off again.

'Much more smoothly than a live horse,' Alice said, with a little scream of laughter, in spite of all she could do to prevent it.

'I'll get one,' the Knight said thoughtfully to himself. 'One or two – several.'

There was a short silence after this, and then the Knight went on again. 'I'm a great hand at inventing things. Now, I dare say you noticed, the last time you picked me up, that I was looking rather thoughtful?'

'You *were* a little grave,' said Alice.

'Well, just then I was inventing a new way of getting over a gate – would you like to hear it?'

'Very much indeed,' Alice said politely.

'I'll tell you how I came to think of it,'said the Knight. 'You see, I said to myself, "The only difficulty is with the feet: the *head* is high enough already." Now, first I put my head on the top of the gate – then the head's high enough – then I stand on my head – then the feet are high enough, you see – then I'm over, you see.'

'Yes, I suppose you'd be over when that was done,' Alice said thoughtfully: 'but don't you think it would be rather hard?'

'I haven't tried it yet,' the Knight said, gravely: 'so I can't tell for certain – but I'm afraid it *would* be a little hard.'

He looked so vexed at the idea, that Alice changed the subject hastily. 'What a curious helmet you've got!' she said cheerfully. 'Is that your invention too?'

The Knight looked down proudly at his helmet, which hung from the saddle. 'Yes,' he said, 'but I've invented a better one than that – like a sugar-loaf. When I used to wear it, if I fell off the horse, it always touched the ground directly. So I had a *very* little way to fall, you see – But there *was* the danger of falling *into* it, to be sure. That happened to me once – and the worst of it was, before I could get out again, the other White Knight came and put it on. He thought it was his own helmet.'

The Knight looked so solemn about it that Alice did not dare to laugh. 'I'm afraid you must have hurt him,' she said in a trembling voice, 'being on the top of his head.'

'I had to kick him, of course,' the Knight said, very seriously. 'And then he took the helmet off again – but it took hours and hours to get me out. I was as fast as – as lightning, you know.'

'But that's a different kind of fastness,' Alice objected.

The Knight shook his head. 'It was all kinds of fastness with me, I can assure you!' he said. He raised his hands in some excitement as he said this, and instantly rolled out of the saddle, and fell headlong into a deep ditch.

Alice ran to the side of the ditch to look for him. She was rather startled by the fall, as for some time he had kept on very well, and she was afraid that he really *was* hurt this time. However, though she could see nothing but the soles of his feet, she was much relieved to hear that he was talking on in his usual tone. 'All kinds of fastness,' he repeated: 'but it was careless of him to put another man's helmet on – with the man in it, too.'

'How *can* you go on talking so quietly, head downwards?' Alice asked, as she dragged him out by the feet, and laid him in a heap on the bank.

The knight looked surprised at the question. 'What does it matter where my body happens to be?' he said. 'My mind goes on working all the same. In fact, the more head-downwards I am, the more I keep inventing new things.

'Now the cleverest thing of the sort that I ever did,' he went on, after a pause, 'was inventing a new pudding during the meat-course.'

'In time to have it cooked for the next course?' said Alice. 'Well, that *was* quick work, certainly.'

'Well, not the *next* course,' the Knight said in a slow, thoughtful tone: 'no certainly not the next *course.*'

'Then it would have to be the next day. I suppose you wouldn't have two pudding-courses in one dinner?'

'Well, not the *next* day,' the Knight repeated as before: 'not the next *day.* In fact,' he went on, holding his head down, and his voice getting lower and lower, 'I don't believe that pudding ever *was* cooked! In fact, I don't believe that pudding ever *will* be cooked! And yet it was a very clever pudding to invent.'

'What did you mean it to be made of?' Alice asked, hoping to cheer him up, for the poor Knight seemed quite low-spirited about it.

'It began with blotting-paper,' the Knight answered with a groan.

'That wouldn't be very nice, I'm afraid –'

'Not very nice *alone*,' he interrupted, quite eagerly; 'but you've no idea what a difference it makes, mixing it with other things – such as gunpowder and sealing-wax. And here I must leave you.' They had just come to the end of the wood.

Alice could only look puzzled: she was thinking of the pudding.

'You are sad,' the Knight said in an anxious tone: 'let me sing you a song to comfort you.'

'Is it very long?' Alice asked, for she had heard a good deal of poetry that day.

'It's long,' said the Knight, 'but it's very, *very* beautiful. Everybody that hears me sing it – either it brings the *tears* into their eyes or else –'

'Or else what?' said Alice, for the Knight had made a sudden pause.

'Or else it doesn't, you know. The name of the song is called "*Haddocks' Eyes*".'

'Oh, that's the name of the song, is it?' Alice said, trying to feel interested.

'No, you don't understand,' the Knight said, looking a little vexed. 'That's what the name is *called*. The name really *is* "*The Aged Aged Man*."'

'Then I ought to have said, "That's what the *song* is called"?' Alice corrected herself.

'No, you oughtn't: that's quite another thing! The *song* is called "*Ways and Means*": but that's only what it's *called*, you know!'

'Well, what *is* the song, then?' said Alice, who was by this time completely bewildered.

'I was coming to that,' the Knight said. 'The song really *is* "*A-sitting On a Gate*": and the tune's my own invention.'

So saying, he stopped his horse and let the reins fall on its neck: then, slowly beating time with one hand, and with a faint smile lighting up his gentle, foolish face, as if he enjoyed the music of his song, he began.

Of all the strange things that Alice saw in her journey Through the Looking-Glass, this was the one that she always remembered most clearly. Years afterwards she could bring the whole scene back again, as if it had been only yesterday – the mild blue eyes and kindly smile of the Knight – the setting sun gleaming through his hair, and shining on his armour in a blaze of light that quite dazzled her – the horse quietly moving about, with the reins hanging loose on his neck, cropping the grass at her feet – and the black shadows of the forest behind – all this she took in like a picture, as, with one hand shading her eyes, she leant against a tree, watching the strange pair, and listening, in a half-dream, to the melancholy music of the song.

'But the tune *isn't* his own invention,' she said to herself: 'it's "*I give thee all, I can no more.*"' She stood and listened very attentively, but no tears came into her eyes.

> *I'll tell thee everything I can;*
> *There's little to relate.*
> *I saw an aged aged man,*
> *A-sitting on the gate.*
> *"Who are you, aged man?" I said.*

"And how is it you live?"
And his answer trickled through my head
Like water through a sieve.

He said, "I look for butterflies
That sleep among the wheat:
I make them into mutton-pies,
And sell them in the street.
I sell them unto men," he said,
"Who sail on stormy seas;
And that's the way I get my bread –
A trifle, if you please."

But I was thinking of a plan
To dye one's whiskers green,
And always use so large a fan
That they could not be seen.
So, having no reply to give
To what the old man said,
I cried, "Come, tell me how you live!"
And thumped him on the head.

His accents mild took up the tale:
He said, "I go my ways,
And when I find a mountain-rill,
I set it in a blaze;
And thence they make a stuff they call
Rowland's Macassar Oil –
Yet twopence-halfpenny is all
They give me for my toil."

But I was thinking of a way
To feed oneself on batter,

And so go on from day to day
Getting a little fatter.
I shook him well from side to side,
Until his face was blue:
"Come, tell me how you live," I cried,
"And what it is you do!"

He said, I hunt for haddocks' eyes
Among the heather bright,
And work them into waistcoat-buttons
In the silent night.
And these I do not sell for gold
Or coin of silvery shine,
But for a copper halfpenny,
And that will purchase nine.

"I sometimes dig for buttered rolls,
Or set limed twigs for crabs;
I sometimes search the grassy knolls
For wheels of Hansom-cabs.
And that's the way" (he gave a wink)
"By which I get my wealth –
And very gladly will I drink
Your Honour's noble health."

I heard him then, for I had just
Completed my design
To keep the Menai bridge from rust
By boiling it in wine.
I thanked him much for telling me
The way he got his wealth,
But chiefly for his wish that he
Might drink my noble health.

And now, if e'er by chance I put
My fingers into glue,
Or madly squeeze a right-hand foot
Into a left-hand shoe,
Or if I drop upon my toe
A very heavy weight,
I weep, for it reminds me so
Of that old man I used to know –
Whose look was mild, whose speech was
slow,
Whose hair was whiter than the snow,
Whose face was very like a crow,
With eyes, like cinders, all aglow,
Who seemed distracted with his woe,
Who rocked his body to and fro,
And muttered mumblingly and low,
As if his mouth were full of dough,
Who snorted like a buffalo –
That summer evening long ago
A-sitting on a gate.'

As the Knight sang the last words of the ballad, he gathered up the reins, and turned his horse's head along the road by which they had come. 'You've only a few yards to go,' he said, 'down the hill and over that little brook, and then you'll be a Queen – But you'll stay and see me off first?' he added, as Alice turned with an eager look in the direction to which he pointed. 'I shan't be long. You'll wait and wave your handkerchief when I get to that turn in the road! I think it'll encourage me, you see.'

'Of course I'll wait,' said Alice: 'and thank you very much for coming so far – and for the song – I liked it very much.'

'I hope so,' the Knight said doubtfully: 'but you didn't cry so much as I thought you would.'

So they shook hands, and then the Knight rode slowly away into the forest. 'It won't take long to see him *off*, I expect,' Alice said to herself, as she stood watching him. 'There he goes! Right on his head as usual! However, he gets on again pretty easily – that comes of having so many things hung round the horse –' So she went on talking to herself, as she watched the horse walking leisurely along the road, and the Knight tumbled off first on one side and then on the other. After the fourth or fifth tumble he reached the turn, and then she waved her handkerchief to him, and waited till he was out of sight.

'I hope it encouraged him,' she said, as she turned to run down the hill: 'and now for the last brook, and to be a Queen! How grand it sounds!' A very few steps

brought her to the edge of the brook. 'The Eighth Square at last!' she cried, as she bounded across, and threw herself down to rest on a lawn as soft as moss, with little flower-beds dotted about it here and there. 'Oh, how glad I am to get here! And what *is* this on my head?' she exclaimed in a tone of dismay, as she put her hands up to something very heavy, that fitted tight all round her head.

'But how *can* it have got there without my knowing it?' she said to herself, as she lifted it off, and set it on her lap to make out what it could possibly be.

It was a golden crown.

CHAPTER 9

Queen Alice

'Well, this *is* grand!' said Alice. 'I never expected I should be a Queen so soon – and I'll tell you what it is, your Majesty,' she went on in a severe tone (she was always rather fond of scolding herself), 'it'll never do for you to be lolling about on the grass like that! Queens have to be dignified, you know!'

So she got up and walked about – rather stiffly just at first, as she was afraid that the crown might come off:

but she comforted herself with the thought that there was nobody to see her, 'and if I really am a Queen,' she said, as she sat down again, 'I shall be able to manage it quite well in time.'

Everything was happening so oddly that she didn't feel a bit surprised at finding the Red Queen and the White Queen sitting close to her, one on each side: she would have liked very much to ask them how they came there, but she feared it would not be quite civil. However, there would be no harm, she thought, in asking if the game was over. 'Please, would you tell me –' she began, looking timidly at the Red Queen.

'Speak when you're spoken to!' the Queen sharply interrupted her.

'But if everybody obeyed that rule!' said Alice, who was always ready for a little argument, 'and if you only spoke when you were spoken to, and the other person always waited for *you* to begin, you see nobody would ever say anything, so that –'

'Ridiculous!' cried the Queen. 'Why, don't you see, child –' here she broke off with a frown, and, after thinking for a minute, suddenly changed the subject of the conversation. 'What do you mean by "If you really are a queen"? What right have you to call yourself so? You can't be a Queen, you know, till you've passed the proper examination. And the sooner we begin it the better.'

'I only said "if"!' poor Alice pleaded in a piteous tone.

The two Queens looked at each other, and the Red Queen remarked with a little shudder, 'She *says* she only said "if" –'

'But she said a great deal more than that!' the White

Queen moaned, wringing her hands. 'Oh, ever so much more than that!'

'So you did, you know,' the Red Queen said to Alice. 'Always speak the truth – think before you speak – and write it down afterwards.'

'I'm sure I didn't mean –' Alice was beginning, but the Red Queen interrupted her impatiently.

'That's just what I complain of! You *should* have meant! What do you suppose is the use of a child without any meaning? Even a joke should have some meaning – and a child's more important than a joke, I hope. You couldn't deny that, even if you tried with both hands.'

'I don't deny things with my *hands*,' Alice objected.

'Nobody said you did,' said the Red Queen. 'I said you couldn't if you tried.'

'She's in that state of mind,' said the White Queen, 'that she wants to deny *something* – only she doesn't know what to deny!'

'A nasty, vicious temper,' the Red Queen remarked; and then there was an uncomfortable silence for a minute or two.

The Red Queen broke the silence by saying to the White Queen, 'I invite you to Alice's dinner-party this afternoon.'

The White Queen smiled feebly, and said, 'And I invite *you*.'

'I didn't know I was to have a party at all,' said Alice; 'but if there *is* to be one, I think *I* ought to invite the guests.'

'We gave you the opportunity of doing it,' the Red Queen remarked: 'but I dare say you've not had many lessons in manners yet?'

'Manners are not taught in lessons,' said Alice. 'Lessons teach you to do sums, and things of that sort.'

'Can you do Addition?' the White Queen asked. 'What's one and one and one and one and one and one and one and one and one and one?'

'I don't know,' said Alice. 'I lost count.'

'She can't do Addition,' the Red Queen interrupted. 'Can you do Subtraction? Take nine from eight.'

'Nine from eight I can't, you know,' Alice replied very readily: 'but –'

'She can't do Subtraction,' said the White Queen. 'Can you do Division? Divide a loaf by a knife – what's the answer to that?'

'I suppose –' Alice was beginning, but the Red Queen answered for her.

'Bread-and-butter, of course. Try another Subtraction sum. Take a bone from a dog. What remains?'

Alice considered. 'The bone wouldn't remain, of course, if I took it – and the dog wouldn't remain: it would come to bite me – and I'm sure *I* shouldn't remain!'

'Then you think nothing would remain?' said the Red Queen.

'I think that's the answer.'

'Wrong, as usual,' said the Red Queen: 'the dog's temper would remain.'

'But I don't see how –'

'Why, look here!' the Red Queen cried. 'The dog would lose its temper, wouldn't it?'

'Perhaps it would,' Alice replied cautiously.

'Then if the dog went away, its temper would remain!' the Queen exclaimed triumphantly.

Alice said as gravely as she could, 'They might go

different ways.' But she couldn't help thinking to herself, 'What dreadful nonsense we *are* talking!'

'She can't do sums a *bit!*' the Queens said together, with great emphasis.

'Can *you* do sums?' Alice said, turning suddenly on the White Queen, for she didn't like being found fault with so much.

The Queen gasped and shut her eyes. 'I can do Addition,' she said, 'if you give me time – but I can't do Subtraction under *any* circumstances!'

'Of course you know your A B C?' said the Red Queen.

'To be sure I do,' said Alice.

'So do I,' the White Queen whispered: 'we'll often say it over together, dear. And I'll tell you a secret – I can read words of one letter! Isn't *that* grand? However, don't be discouraged. You'll come to it in time.'

Here the Red Queen began again. 'Can you answer useful questions?' she said. 'How is bread made?'

'I know *that!*' Alice cried eagerly. 'You take some flour –'

'Where do you pick the flower?' the White Queen asked. 'In a garden, or in the hedges?'

'Well, it isn't *picked* at all,' Alice explained: 'it's *ground* –'

'How many acres of ground?' said the White Queen. 'You mustn't leave out so many things.'

'Fan her head!' the Red Queen anxiously interrupted. 'She'll be feverish after so much thinking.' So they set to work and fanned her with bunches of leaves, till she had to beg them to leave off, it blew her hair about so.

'She's all right again now,' said the Red Queen. 'Do

you know Languages? What's the French for "Fiddle-de-dee"?'

'Fiddle-de-dee's not English,' Alice replied gravely.

'Who ever said it was?' said the Red Queen.

Alice thought she saw a way out of the difficulty this time. 'If you'll tell me what language "fiddle-de-dee" is, I'll tell you the French for it!' she exclaimed triumphantly.

But the Red Queen drew herself up rather stiffly, and said, 'Queens never make bargains.'

'I wish Queens never asked questions,' Alice thought to herself.

'Don't let us quarrel,' the White Queen said in an anxious tone. 'What is the cause of lightning?'

'The cause of lightning,' Alice said very decidedly, for she felt quite certain about this, 'is the thunder – no, no!' she hastily corrected herself. 'I meant the other way.'

'It's too late to correct it,' said the Red Queen: 'when you've once said a thing, that fixes it, and you must take the consequences.'

'Which reminds me' – the White Queen said, looking down and nervously clasping and unclasping her hands –' we had *such* a thunderstorm last Tuesday – I mean one of the last set of Tuesdays, you know.'

Alice was puzzled. 'In our country,' she remarked, 'there's only one day at a time.'

The Red Queen said, 'That's a poor thin way of doing things. Now *here*, we mostly have days and nights two or three at a time and sometimes in the winter we take as many as five nights together – for warmth, you know.'

'Are five nights warmer than one night, then?' Alice ventured to ask.

'Five times as warm, of course.'

'But they should be five times as *cold*, by the same rule –'

'Just so!' cried the Red Queen. 'Five times as warm, *and* five times as cold – just as I'm five times as rich as you are, *and* five times as clever!'

Alice sighed and gave it up. 'It's exactly like a riddle with no answer!' she thought.

'Humpty Dumpty saw it too,' the White Queen went on in a low voice, more as if she were talking to herself. 'He came to the door with a corkscrew in his hand –'

'What did he want?' said the Red Queen.

'He said he *would* come in,' the White Queen went on, 'because he was looking for a hippopotamus. Now, as it happened there wasn't such a thing in the house that morning.'

'Is there generally?' Alice asked in an astonished tone.

'Well, only on Thursdays,' said the Queen.

'I knew what he came for,' said Alice: 'he wanted to punish the fish, because –'

Here the White Queen began again. 'It was *such* a thunderstorm, you can't think!' ('She *never* could, you know,' said the Red Queen.) 'And part of the roof came off, and ever so much thunder got in – and it went rolling round the room in great lumps – and knocking over the tables and things – till I was so frightened I couldn't remember my own name!'

Alice thought to herself, 'I never should *try* to remember my name in the middle of an accident! Where would be the use of it?' But she did not say this aloud, for fear of hurting the poor Queen's feelings.

'Your Majesty must excuse her,' the Red Queen said to Alice, taking one of the White Queen's hands in her own, and gently stroking it: 'she means well, but she can't help saying foolish things, as a general rule.'

The White Queen looked timidly at Alice, who felt she *ought* to say something kind, but really couldn't think of anything at the moment.

'She never was really well brought up,' the Red Queen went on: 'but it's amazing how good-tempered she is! Pat her on the head and see how pleased she'll be!' But this was more than Alice had courage to do.

'A little kindness – and putting her hair in papers – would do wonders with her –'

The White Queen gave a deep sigh, and laid her head on Alice's shoulder. 'I *am* so sleepy!' she moaned.

'She's tired, poor thing!' said the Red Queen. 'Smooth her hair – lend her your nightcap – and sing her a soothing lullaby.'

'I haven't got a nightcap with me,' said Alice, as she tried to obey the first direction: 'and I don't know any soothing lullabies.'

'I must do it myself, then,' said the Red Queen, and she began:

> *'Hush-a-by lady, in Alice's lap!*
> *Till the feast's ready we've time for a nap:*
> *When the feast's over, we'll go to the ball –*
> *Red Queen, and White Queen, and Alice,*
> > *and all!*

'And now you know the words,' she added, as she put her head down on Alice's other shoulder, 'just sing it through to *me*. I'm getting sleepy, too.' In another moment both Queens were fast asleep, and snoring loud.

'What *am* I to do?' exclaimed Alice, looking about in great perplexity, as first one round head, and then the other, rolled down from her shoulder, and lay like a heavy lump in her lap. 'I don't think it *ever* happened before, that any one had to take care of two Queens asleep at once! No, not in all the History of England – it couldn't, you know, because there never was more than one Queen at a time. Do wake up, you heavy things!' she went on in an impatient tone; but there was no answer but a gentle snoring.

The snoring got more distinct every minute, and sounded more like a tune: at last she could even make out words, and she listened so eagerly that, when the two great heads suddenly vanished from her lap, she hardly missed them.

She was standing before an arched doorway, over which were the words QUEEN ALICE in large letters, and on each side of the arch there was a bell-handle; one was marked 'Visitors' Bell,' and the other 'Servants' Bell.'

'I'll wait till the song's over,' thought Alice, 'and then I'll ring the – the – *which* bell must I ring?' she went on, very much puzzled by the names. 'I'm not a

visitor, and I'm not a servant. There *ought* to be one marked "Queen," you know –'

Just then the door opened a little way, and a creature with a long beak put its head out for a moment and said, 'No admittance till the week after next!' and shut the door again with a bang.

Alice knocked and rang in vain for a long time: but at last a very old Frog, who was sitting under a tree, got up and hobbled slowly towards her: he was dressed in bright yellow, and had enormous boots on.

'What is it, now?' the Frog said in a deep, hoarse whisper.

Alice turned round, ready to find fault with anybody. 'Where's the servant whose business it is to answer the door?' she began angrily.

'Which door?' said the Frog.

Alice almost stamped with irritation at the slow drawl in which he spoke. '*This* door, of course!'

The Frog looked at the door with his large dull eyes for a minute: then he went nearer and rubbed it with his thumb, as if he were trying whether the paint would come off; then he looked at Alice.

'To answer the door?' he said. 'What's it been asking of?'

He was so hoarse that Alice could scarcely hear him.

'I don't know what you mean,' she said.

'I speaks English, doesn't I?' the Frog went on. 'Or are you deaf? What did it ask you?'

'Nothing!' Alice said impatiently. 'I've been knocking at it!'

'Shouldn't do that – shouldn't do that –' the Frog muttered. 'Wexes it, you know.' Then he went up and gave the door a kick with one of his great feet. 'You let *it* alone,' he panted out, as he hobbled back to his tree, 'and it'll let *you* alone, you know.'

At this moment the door was flung open, and a shrill voice was heard singing:

> '*To the Looking-Glass world it was Alice that said,*
> "*I've a sceptre in hand, I've a crown on my head;*
> *Let the Looking-Glass creatures, whatever they be,*
> *Come and dine with the Red Queen, the White Queen, and me!*"'

And hundreds of voices joined in the chorus:

> *'Then fill up the glasses as quick as you can,*
> *And sprinkle the table with buttons and bran:*
> *Put cats in the coffee, and mice in the tea –*
> *And welcome Queen Alice with thirty-*
> *times-three!'*

Then followed a confused noise of cheering, and Alice thought to herself, 'Thirty times three makes ninety. I wonder if any one's counting?' In a minute there was silence again, and the same shrill voice sang another verse:

> *"'O Looking-Glass creatures," quoth Alice,*
> *"draw near!*
> *'Tis an honour to see me, a favour to hear:*
> *'Tis a privilege high to have dinner and tea*
> *Along with the Red Queen, the White*
> *Queen, and me!'*

Then came the chorus again:

> *'Then fill up the glasses with treacle and ink,*
> *Or anything else that is pleasant to drink;*
> *Mix sand with the cider, and wool with the*
> *wine –*
> *And welcome Queen Alice with ninety-*
> *times-nine!'*

'Ninety times nine!' Alice repeated in despair. 'Oh, that'll never be done! I'd better go in at once' – and in she went, and there was a dead silence the moment she appeared.

Alice glanced nervously along the table, as she walked up the large hall, and noticed that there were about fifty guests, of all kinds: some were animals, some

birds, and there were even a few flowers among them.
'I'm glad they've come without waiting to be asked,' she
thought: 'I should never have known who were the right
people to invite.'

There were three chairs at the head of the table; the
Red and White Queens had already taken two of them,
but the middle one was empty. Alice sat down in it,
rather uncomfortable at the silence, and longing for some
one to speak.

At last the Red Queen began. 'You've missed the
soup and fish,' she said. 'Put on the joint!' And the waiters
set a leg of mutton before Alice, who looked at it rather
anxiously, as she had never had to carve a joint before.

'You look a little shy; let me introduce you to that
leg of mutton,' said the Red Queen. 'Alice – Mutton;
Mutton – Alice.' The leg of mutton got up in the dish
and made a little bow to Alice; and Alice returned the
bow, not knowing whether to be frightened or amused.

'May I give you a slice?' she said, taking up the knife and fork, and looking from one Queen to the other.

'Certainly not,' the Red Queen said very decidedly: 'it isn't etiquette to cut any one you've been introduced to. Remove the joint!' And the waiters carried it off, and brought large plum pudding in its place.

'I won't be introduced to the pudding, please,' Alice cried, rather hastily, 'or we shall get no dinner at all. May I give you some?'

But the Red Queen looked sulky, and growled, 'Pudding – Alice; Alice – Pudding. Remove the pudding!' and the waiters took it away so quickly that Alice couldn't return its bow.

However, she didn't see why the Red Queen should be the only one to give orders, so, as an experiment, she called out, 'Waiter! Bring back the pudding!' and there it was again in a moment, like a conjuring trick. It was so large that she couldn't help feeling a *little* shy with it, as she had been with the mutton; however, she conquered her shyness by a great effort, and cut a slice and handed it to the Red Queen.

'What impertinence!' said the Pudding. 'I wonder how you'd like it, if I were to cut a slice out of *you*, you creature!'

It spoke in a thick, suety sort of voice, and Alice hadn't a word to say in reply: she could only sit and look at it and gasp.

'Make a remark,' said the Red Queen: 'it's ridiculous to leave all the conversation to the pudding!'

'Do you know, I've had such a quantity of poetry repeated to me today,' Alice began, a little frightened at finding that, the moment she opened her lips, there was dead silence, and all eyes were fixed upon her; 'and it's a very curious thing, I think – every poem was about fishes in some way. Do you know why they're so fond of fishes, all about here?'

She spoke to the Red Queen, whose answer was a little wide of the mark. 'As to fishes,' she said, very slowly and solemnly, putting her mouth close to Alice's ear, 'her White Majesty knows a lovely riddle – all in poetry – all about fishes. Shall she repeat it?'

'Her Red Majesty's very kind to mention it,' the White Queen murmured into Alice's other ear, in a voice like the cooing of a pigeon. 'It would be *such* a treat! May I?'

'Please do,' Alice said very politely.

The White Queen laughed with delight, and stroked Alice's cheek. Then she began:

> *"First the fish must be caught."*
> *That is easy: a baby, I think, could have*
> * caught it.*
> *"Next, the fish must be bought.'*
> *That is easy: a penny, I think, would have*
> * bought it.*
>
> *"Now cook me the fish!*
> *That is easy, and will not take more than a*
> * minute.*
> *"Let it lie in a dish!"*
> *That is easy, because it already is in it.*
>
> *"Bring it here! Let me sup!"*
> *It is easy to set such a dish on the table.*
> *"Take the dish-cover up!"*
> *Ah, that is so hard that I fear I'm unable!*

> *For it holds it like glue –*
> *Holds the lid to the dish, while it lies in the*
> *middle:*
> *Which is easiest to do,*
> *Un-dish-cover the fish, or dishcover the*
> *riddle?'*

'Take a minute to think about it, and then guess,' said the Red Queen. 'Meanwhile, we'll drink your health – Queen Alice's health!' she screamed at the top of her voice, and all the guests began drinking it directly, and very queerly they managed it: some of them put their glasses upon their heads like extinguishers, and drank all that trickled down their faces – others upset the decanters, and drank the wine as it ran off the edges of the table – and three of them (who looked like kanga-roos) scrambled into the dish of roast mutton, and began eagerly lapping up the gravy, 'just like pigs in a trough!' thought Alice.

'You ought to return thanks in a neat speech,' the Red Queen said, frowning at Alice as she spoke.

'We must support you, you know,' the White Queen whispered, as Alice got up to do it, very obediently, but a little frightened.

'Thank you very much,' she whispered in reply, 'but I can do quite well without.'

'That wouldn't be at all the thing,' the Red Queen said very decidedly: so Alice tried to submit to it with a good grace.

('And they *did* push so!' she said afterwards, when she was telling her sister the history of the feast. 'You would have thought they wanted to squeeze me flat!')

In fact it was rather difficult for her to keep in her

place while she made her speech: the two Queens pushed her so, one on each side, that they nearly lifted her up into the air. 'I rise to return thanks –' Alice began: and she really *did* rise as she spoke, several inches; but she got hold of the edge of the table, and managed to pull herself down again.

'Take care of yourself!' screamed the White Queen, seizing Alice's hair with both her hands. 'Something's going to happen!'

And then (as Alice afterwards described it) all sorts of things happened in a moment. The candles all grew up to the ceiling, looking something like a bed of rushes with fireworks at the top. As to the bottles, they each took a pair of plates, which they hastily fitted on as wings, and so, with forks for legs, went fluttering about in all directions: 'and very like birds they look,' Alice thought to herself, as well as she could in the dreadful confusion that was beginning.

At this moment she heard a hoarse laugh at her side, and turned to see what was the matter with the White Queen; but, instead of the Queen, there was the leg of mutton sitting in the chair. 'Here I am!' cried a voice from the soup-tureen, and Alice turned again, just in time to see the Queen's broad, good-natured face grinning at her for a moment over the edge of the tureen, before she disappeared into the soup.

There was not a moment to be lost. Already several of the guests were lying down in the dishes, and the soup-ladle was walking up the table towards Alice's chair, and beckoning to her impatiently to get out of its way.

'I can't stand this any longer!' she cried, as she

jumped up and seized the tablecloth with both hands: one good pull, and plates, dishes, guests, and candles came crashing down together in a heap on the floor.

'And as for *you*,' she went on, turning fiercely upon the Red Queen, whom she considered as the cause of all the mischief – but the Queen was no longer at her side – she had suddenly dwindled down to the size of a little doll, and was now on the table, merrily running round and round after her own shawl, which was trailing behind her.

At any other time, Alice would have felt surprised at this, but she was far too much excited to be surprised at anything *now*. 'As for *you*,' she repeated, catching hold of the little creature in the very act of jumping over a bottle which had just lighted upon the table, 'I'll shake you into a kitten, that I will!'

CHAPTER 10

Shaking

She took her off the table as she spoke, and shook her backwards and forwards with all her might.

The Red Queen made no resistance whatever: only

her face grew very small, and her eyes got large and green: and still, as Alice went on shaking her, she kept on growing shorter – and fatter – and softer – and rounder – and –

CHAPTER 11

Waking

– and it really was a kitten, after all.

CHAPTER 12

Which Dreamed It?

'Your Red Majesty shouldn't purr so loud,' Alice said, rubbing her eyes, and addressing the kitten respectfully, yet with some severity. 'You woke me out of – oh! such a nice dream! And you've been along with me, Kitty – all through the Looking-Glass world. Did you know it, dear?'

It is a very convenient habit of kittens (Alice had once made the remark) that, whatever you say to them, they *always* purr. 'If they would only purr for "yes," and mew for "no," or any rule of that sort,' she had said, 'so that one could keep up a conversation! But how *can* you talk with a person if they always say the same thing?'

On this occasion the kitten only purred: and it was impossible to guess whether it meant 'yes' or 'no.'

So Alice hunted among the chessmen on the table till she had found the Red Queen: then she went down on her knees on the hearthrug, and put the kitten and the Queen to look at each other. 'Now, Kitty!' she cried, clapping her hands triumphantly. 'Confess that was what you turned into!'

('But it wouldn't look at it,' she said, when she was explaining the thing afterwards to her sister: 'it turned away its head, and pretended not to see it: but it looked a *little* ashamed of itself, so I think it *must* have been the Red Queen').

'Sit up a little more stiffly, dear!' Alice cried, with a merry laugh. 'And curtsey while you're thinking what to – what to purr. It saves time, remember!' And she caught it up and gave it one little kiss, 'just in honour of its having been a Red Queen.'

'Snowdrop, my pet!' she went on, looking over her shoulder at the White Kitten, which was still patiently undergoing its toilet, 'when *will* Dinah have finished with your White Majesty, I wonder? That must be the reason you were so untidy in my dream – Dinah! Do you know that you're scrubbing a White Queen? Really, it's most disrespectful of you.

'And what did *Dinah* turn to, I wonder?' she prattled on, as she settled comfortably down, with one elbow on the rug, and her chin in her hand, to watch the kittens. 'Tell me, Dinah, did you turn to Humpty Dumpty? I *think* you did – however, you'd better not mention it to your friends just yet, for I'm not sure.

'By the way, Kitty, if only you'd been really with me in my dream, there was one thing you *would* have enjoyed – I had such a quantity of poetry said to me, all about fishes! Tomorrow morning you shall have a real treat. All the time you're eating your breakfast, I'll repeat "The Walrus and the Carpenter" to you; and then you can make believe it's oysters, dear!

'Now, Kitty, let's consider who it was that dreamed it all. This is a serious question, my dear, and you should *not* go on licking your paw like that – as if Dinah hadn't washed you this morning! You see, Kitty, it *must* have been either me or the Red King. He was part of my dream, of course – but then I was part of his dream, too! *Was* it the Red King, Kitty? You were his wife, my dear, so you ought to know – Oh, Kitty, *do* help to settle it! I'm sure your paw can wait!' But the provoking kitten only began on the other paw and pretended it hadn't heard the question.

Which do *you* think it was?

AFTERWORD

A boat,* beneath a sunny sky
Lingering onward dreamily
In an evening of July –

Children three that nestle near,
Eager eye and willing ear,
Pleased a simple tale to hear –

Long has paled that sunny sky:
Echoes fade and memories die:
Autumn frosts have slain July.

Still she haunts me, phantomwise.
Alice moving under skies
Never seen by waking eyes.

Children yet, the tale to hear,
Eager eye and willing ear,
Lovingly shall nestle near.

> *In a Wonderland they lie,*
> *Dreaming as the days go by,*
> *Dreaming as the summers die:*
>
> *Ever drifting down the stream –*
> *Lingering in the golden gleam –*
> *Life, what is it but a dream?*

The first letter of each line of this poem, put together, read ALICE PLEASANCE LIDDELL the full name of Dean Liddell's second daughter, the 'real' Alice.

Classic Literature: Words and Phrases
*adapted from the **Collins English Dictionary***

Accoucheur NOUN a male midwife or doctor ❑ *I think my sister must have had some general idea that I was a young offender whom an Accoucheur Policemen had taken up (on my birthday) and delivered over to her* (*Great Expectations* by Charles Dickens)

addled ADJ confused and unable to think properly ❑ *But she counted and counted till she got that addled* (*The Adventures of Huckleberry Finn* by Mark Twain)

admiration NOUN amazement or wonder ❑ *lifting up his hands and eyes by way of admiration* (*Gulliver's Travels* by Jonathan Swift)

afeard ADJ afeard means afraid ❑ *shake it – and don't be afeard* (*The Adventures of Huckleberry Finn* by Mark Twain)

affected VERB affected means followed ❑ *Hadst thou affected sweet divinity* (*Doctor Faustus 5.2* by Christopher Marlowe)

aground ADV when a boat runs aground, it touches the ground in a shallow part of the water and gets stuck ❑ *what kep' you? – boat get aground?* (*The Adventures of Huckleberry Finn* by Mark Twain)

ague NOUN a fever in which the patient has alternate hot and cold shivering fits ❑ *his exposure to the wet and cold had brought on fever and ague* (*Oliver Twist* by Charles Dickens)

alchemy ADJ false or worthless ❑ *all wealth alchemy* (*The Sun Rising* by John Donne)

all alike phrase the same all the time ❑ *Love, all alike* (*The Sun Rising* by John Donne)

alow and aloft phrase alow means in the lower part or bottom, and aloft means on the top, so alow and aloft means on the top and in the bottom or throughout ❑ *Someone's turned the chest out alow and aloft* (*Treasure Island* by Robert Louis Stevenson)

ambuscade NOUN ambuscade is not a proper word. Tom means an ambush, which is when a group of people attack their enemies, after hiding and waiting for them ❑ *and so we would lie in ambuscade, as he called it* (*The Adventures of Huckleberry Finn* by Mark Twain)

amiable ADJ likeable or pleasant ❑ *Such amiable qualities must speak for themselves* (*Pride and Prejudice* by Jane Austen)

amulet NOUN an amulet is a charm thought to drive away evil spirits. ❑ *uttered phrases at once occult and familiar, like the amulet worn on the heart* (*Silas Marner* by George Eliot)

amusement NOUN here amusement means a strange and disturbing puzzle ❑ *this was an amusement the other way* (*Robinson Crusoe* by Daniel Defoe)

ancient NOUN an ancient was the flag displayed on a ship to show which country it belongs to. It is also called the ensign ❑ *her ancient and pendants out* (*Robinson Crusoe* by Daniel Defoe)

antic ADJ here antic means horrible or grotesque ❑ *armed and dressed after a very antic manner* (*Gulliver's Travels* by Jonathan Swift)

antics NOUN antics is an old word meaning clowns, or people who do silly things to make other people laugh ❑ *And point like antics at his triple crown* (*Doctor Faustus 3.2* by Christopher Marlowe)

appanage NOUN an appanage is a living allowance ❑ *As if loveliness were not the special prerogative of woman*

– her legitimate appanage and heritage! (Jane Eyre by Charlotte Brontë)

appended VERB appended means attached or added to ❏ *and these words appended* (Treasure Island by Robert Louis Stevenson)

approver NOUN an approver is someone who gives evidence against someone he used to work with ❏ *Mr. Noah Claypole: receiving a free pardon from the Crown in consequence of being admitted approver against Fagin* (Oliver Twist by Charles Dickens)

areas NOUN the areas is the space, below street level, in front of the basement of a house ❏ *The Dodger had a vicious propensity, too, of pulling the caps from the heads of small boys and tossing them down areas* (Oliver Twist by Charles Dickens)

argument NOUN theme or important idea or subject which runs through a piece of writing ❏ *Thrice needful to the argument which now* (The Prelude by William Wordsworth)

artificially ADJ artfully or cleverly ❏ *and he with a sharp flint sharpened very artificially* (Gulliver's Travels by Jonathan Swift)

artist NOUN here artist means a skilled workman ❏ *This man was a most ingenious artist* (Gulliver's Travels by Jonathan Swift)

assizes NOUN assizes were regular court sessions which a visiting judge was in charge of ❏ *you shall hang at the next assizes* (Treasure Island by Robert Louis Stevenson)

attraction NOUN gravitation, or Newton's theory of gravitation ❏ *he predicted the same fate to attraction* (Gulliver's Travels by Jonathan Swift)

aver VERB to aver is to claim something strongly ❏ *for Jem Rodney, the mole catcher, averred that one evening as he was returning homeward* (Silas Marner by George Eliot)

baby NOUN here baby means doll, which is a child's toy that looks like a small person ❏ *and skilful dressing her baby* (Gulliver's Travels by Jonathan Swift)

bagatelle NOUN bagatelle is a game rather like billiards and pool ❏ *Breakfast had been ordered at a pleasant little tavern, a mile or so away upon the rising ground beyond the green; and there was a bagatelle board in the room, in case we should desire to unbend our minds after the solemnity.* (Great Expectations by Charles Dickens)

bah exclam Bah is an exclamation of frustration or anger ❏ *"Bah," said Scrooge.* (A Christmas Carol by Charles Dickens)

bairn NOUN a northern word for child ❏ *Who has taught you those fine words, my bairn?* (Wuthering Heights by Emily Brontë)

bait VERB to bait means to stop on a journey to take refreshment ❏ *So, when they stopped to bait the horse, and ate and drank and enjoyed themselves, I could touch nothing that they touched, but kept my fast unbroken.* (David Copperfield by Charles Dickens)

balustrade NOUN a balustrade is a row of vertical columns that form railings ❏ *but I mean to say you might have got a hearse up that staircase, and taken it broadwise, with the splinter-bar towards the wall, and the door towards the balustrades: and done it easy* (A Christmas Carol by Charles Dickens)

bandbox NOUN a large lightweight box for carrying bonnets or hats ❏ *I am glad I bought my bonnet, if it is only for the fun of having another bandbox* (Pride and Prejudice by Jane Austen)

barren NOUN a barren here is a stretch or expanse of barren land ❏ *a line of upright stones, continued the length of the barren* (Wuthering Heights by Emily Brontë)

basin NOUN a basin was a cup without a handle ❏ *who is drinking his tea* out of a basin (*Wuthering Heights* by Emily Brontë)

battalia NOUN the order of battle ❏ *till I saw part of his army in battalia* (*Gulliver's Travels* by Jonathan Swift)

battery NOUN a Battery is a fort or a place where guns are positioned ❏ *You bring the lot to me, at that old Battery over yonder* (*Great Expectations* by Charles Dickens)

battledore and shuttlecock NOUN The game battledore and shuttlecock was an early version of the game now known as badminton. The aim of the early game was simply to keep the shuttlecock from hitting the ground. ❏ *Battledore and shuttlecock's a wery good game vhen you an't the shuttlecock and two lawyers the battledores, in which case it gets too excitin' to be pleasant* (*Pickwick Papers* by Charles Dickens)

beadle NOUN a beadle was a local official who had power over the poor ❏ *But these impertinences were speedily checked by the evidence of the surgeon, and the testimony of the beadle* (*Oliver Twist* by Charles Dickens)

bearings NOUN the bearings of a place are the measurements or directions that are used to find or locate it ❏ *the bearings of the island* (*Treasure Island* by Robert Louis Stevenson)

beaufet NOUN a beaufet was a sideboard ❏ *and sweet-cake from the beaufet* (*Emma* by Jane Austen)

beck NOUN a beck is a small stream ❏ *a beck which follows the bend of the glen* (*Wuthering Heights* by Emily Brontë)

bedight VERB decorated ❏ *and bedight with Christmas holly stuck into the top.* (*A Christmas Carol* by Charles Dickens)

Bedlam NOUN Bedlam was a lunatic asylum in London which had statues carved by Caius Gabriel Cibber at its entrance ❏ *Bedlam, and those carved maniacs at the gates* (*The Prelude* by William Wordsworth)

beeves NOUN oxen or castrated bulls which are animals used for pulling vehicles or carrying things ❏ *to deliver in every morning six beeves* (*Gulliver's Travels* by Jonathan Swift)

begot VERB created or caused ❏ *Begot in thee* (*On His Mistress* by John Donne)

behoof NOUN behoof means benefit ❏ *"Yes, young man," said he, releasing the handle of the article in question, retiring a step or two from my table, and speaking for the behoof of the landlord and waiter at the door* (*Great Expectations* by Charles Dickens)

berth NOUN a berth is a bed on a boat ❏ *this is the berth for me* (*Treasure Island* by Robert Louis Stevenson)

bevers NOUN a bever was a snack, or small portion of food, eaten between main meals ❏ *that buys me thirty meals a day and ten bevers* (*Doctor Faustus 2.1* by Christopher Marlowe)

bilge water NOUN the bilge is the widest part of a ship's bottom, and the bilge water is the dirty water that collects there ❏ *no gush of bilge-water had turned it to fetid puddle* (*Jane Eyre* by Charlotte Brontë)

bills NOUN bills is an old term meaning prescription. A prescription is the piece of paper on which your doctor writes an order for medicine and which you give to a chemist to get the medicine ❏ *Are not thy bills hung up as monuments* (*Doctor Faustus 1.1* by Christopher Marlowe)

black cap NOUN a judge wore a black cap when he was about to sentence a prisoner to death ❏ *The judge assumed the black cap, and the prisoner still stood with the same air and gesture.* (*Oliver Twist* by Charles Dickens)

black gentleman NOUN this was another word for the devil ❏ *for she is as impatient as the black gentleman* (*Emma* by Jane Austen)

boot-jack NOUN a wooden device to help take boots off ❏ *The speaker appeared to throw a boot-jack, or some such article, at the person he addressed* (*Oliver Twist* by Charles Dickens)

booty NOUN booty means treasure or prizes ❏ *would be inclined to give up their booty in payment of the dead man's debts* (*Treasure Island* by Robert Louis Stevenson)

Bow Street runner phrase Bow Street runners were the first British police force, set up by the author Henry Fielding in the eighteenth century ❏ *as would have convinced a judge or a Bow Street runner* (*Treasure Island* by Robert Louis Stevenson)

brawn NOUN brawn is a dish of meat which is set in jelly ❏ *Heaped up upon the floor, to form a kind of throne, were turkeys, geese, game, poultry, brawn, great joints of meat, sucking-pigs* (*A Christmas Carol* by Charles Dickens)

bray VERB when a donkey brays, it makes a loud, harsh sound ❏ *and she doesn't bray like a jackass* (*The Adventures of Huckleberry Finn* by Mark Twain)

break VERB in order to train a horse you first have to break it ❏ *"If a high-mettled creature like this," said he, "can't be broken by fair means, she will never be good for anything"* (*Black Beauty* by Anna Sewell)

bullyragging VERB bullyragging is an old word which means bullying. To bullyrag someone is to threaten or force someone to do something they don't want to do ❏ *and a lot of loafers bullyragging him for sport* (*The Adventures of Huckleberry Finn* by Mark Twain)

but prep except for (this) ❏ *but this, all pleasures fancies be* (*The Good-Morrow* by John Donne)

by hand phrase by hand was a common expression of the time meaning that baby had been fed either using a spoon or a bottle rather than by breast-feeding ❏ *My sister, Mrs. Joe Gargery, was more than twenty years older than I, and had established a great reputation with herself . . . because she had bought me up 'by hand'* (*Great Expectations* by Charles Dickens)

bye-spots NOUN bye-spots are lonely places ❏ *and bye-spots of tales rich with indigenous produce* (*The Prelude* by William Wordsworth)

calico NOUN calico is plain white fabric made from cotton ❏ *There was two old dirty calico dresses* (*The Adventures of Huckleberry Finn* by Mark Twain)

camp-fever NOUN camp-fever was another word for the disease typhus ❏ *during a severe camp-fever* (*Emma* by Jane Austen)

cant NOUN cant is insincere or empty talk ❏ *"Man," said the Ghost, "if man you be in heart, not adamant, forbear that wicked cant until you have discovered What the surplus is, and Where it is."* (*A Christmas Carol* by Charles Dickens)

canty ADJ canty means lively, full of life ❏ *My mother lived til eighty, a canty dame to the last* (*Wuthering Heights* by Emily Brontë)

canvas VERB to canvas is to discuss ❏ *We think so very differently on this point Mr Knightley, that there can be no use in canvassing it* (*Emma* by Jane Austen)

capital ADJ capital means excellent or extremely good ❏ *for it's capital, so shady, light, and big* (*Little Women* by Louisa May Alcott)

capstan NOUN a capstan is a device used on a ship to lift sails and anchors ❏ *capstans going, ships going out to sea, and unintelligible sea creatures roaring curses over the bulwarks at respondent lightermen* (*Great Expectations* by Charles Dickens)

case-bottle NOUN a square bottle designed to fit with others into a case ❏ *The spirit being set before him in a huge case-bottle, which had originally come out of some* *ship's locker* (*The Old Curiosity Shop* by Charles Dickens)

casement NOUN casement is a word meaning window. The teacher in Nicholas Nickleby misspells window showing what a bad teacher he is ❏ *W-i-n, win, d-e-r, der, winder, a casement.'* (*Nicholas Nickleby* by Charles Dickens)

cataleptic ADJ a cataleptic fit is one in which the victim goes into a trancelike state and remains still for a long time ❏ *It was at this point in their history that Silas's cataleptic fit occurred during the prayer-meeting* (*Silas Marner* by George Eliot)

cauldron NOUN a cauldron is a large cooking pot made of metal ❏ *stirring a large cauldron which seemed to be full of soup* (*Alice's Adventures in Wonderland* by Lewis Carroll)

cephalic ADJ cephalic means to do with the head ❏ *with ink composed of a cephalic tincture* (*Gulliver's Travels* by Jonathan Swift)

chaise and four NOUN a closed four-wheel carriage pulled by four horses ❏ *he came down on Monday in a chaise and four to see the place* (*Pride and Prejudice* by Jane Austen)

chamberlain NOUN the main servant in a household ❏ *In those times a bed was always to be got there at any hour of the night, and the chamberlain, letting me in at his ready wicket, lighted the candle next in order on his shelf* (*Great Expectations* by Charles Dickens)

characters NOUN distinguishing marks ❏ *Impressed upon all forms the characters* (*The Prelude* by William Wordsworth)

chary ADJ cautious ❏ *I should have been chary of discussing my guardian too freely even with her* (*Great Expectations* by Charles Dickens)

cherishes VERB here cherishes means cheers or brightens ❏ *some*

philosophic song of Truth that cherishes our daily life (*The Prelude* by William Wordsworth)

chickens' meat phrase chickens' meat is an old term which means chickens' feed or food ❏ *I had shook a bag of chickens' meat out in that place* (*Robinson Crusoe* by Daniel Defoe)

chimeras NOUN a chimera is an unrealistic idea or a wish which is unlikely to be fulfilled ❏ *with many other wild impossible chimeras* (*Gulliver's Travels* by Jonathan Swift)

chines NOUN chine is a cut of meat that includes part or all of the backbone of the animal ❏ *and they found hams and chines uncut* (*Silas Marner* by George Eliot)

chits NOUN chits is a slang word which means girls ❏ *I hate affected, niminy-piminy chits!* (*Little Women* by Louisa May Alcott)

chopped VERB chopped means come suddenly or accidentally ❏ *if I had chopped upon them* (*Robinson Crusoe* by Daniel Defoe)

chute NOUN a narrow channel ❏ *One morning about day-break, I found a canoe and crossed over a chute to the main shore* (*The Adventures of Huckleberry Finn* by Mark Twain)

circumspection NOUN careful observation of events and circumstances; caution ❏ *I honour your circumspection* (*Pride and Prejudice* by Jane Austen)

clambered VERB clambered means to climb somewhere with difficulty, usually using your hands and your feet ❏ *he clambered up and down stairs* (*Treasure Island* by Robert Louis Stevenson)

clime NOUN climate ❏ *no season knows nor clime* (*The Sun Rising* by John Donne)

clinched VERB clenched ❏ *the tops whereof I could but just reach with my fist clinched* (*Gulliver's Travels* by Jonathan Swift)

close chair NOUN a close chair is a sedan chair, which is an covered chair which has room for one person. The sedan chair is carried on two poles by two men, one in front and one behind ❑ *persuaded even the Empress herself to let me hold her in her close chair* (*Gulliver's Travels* by Jonathan Swift)

clown NOUN clown here means peasant or person who lives off the land ❑ *In ancient days by emperor and clown* (*Ode on a Nightingale* by John Keats)

coalheaver NOUN a coalheaver loaded coal onto ships using a spade ❑ *Good, strong, wholesome medicine, as was given with great success to two Irish labourers and a coalheaver* (*Oliver Twist* by Charles Dickens)

coal-whippers NOUN men who worked at docks using machines to load coal onto ships ❑ *here, were colliers by the score and score, with the coal-whippers plunging off stages on deck* (*Great Expectations* by Charles Dickens)

cobweb NOUN a cobweb is the net which a spider makes for catching insects ❑ *the walls and ceilings were all hung round with cobwebs* (*Gulliver's Travels* by Jonathan Swift)

coddling VERB coddling means to treat someone too kindly or protect them too much ❑ *and I've been coddling the fellow as if I'd been his grandmother* (*Little Women* by Louisa May Alcott)

coil NOUN coil means noise or fuss or disturbance ❑ *What a coil is there?* (*Doctor Faustus 4.7* by Christopher Marlowe)

collared VERB to collar something is a slang term which means to capture. In this sentence, it means he stole it [the money] ❑ *he collared it* (*The Adventures of Huckleberry Finn* by Mark Twain)

colling VERB colling is an old word which means to embrace and kiss ❑ *and no clasping and colling at all* (*Tess of the D'Urbervilles* by Thomas Hardy)

colloquies NOUN colloquy is a formal conversation or dialogue ❑ *Such colloquies have occupied many a pair of pale-faced weavers* (*Silas Marner* by George Eliot)

comfit NOUN sugar-covered pieces of fruit or nut eaten as sweets ❑ *and pulled out a box of comfits* (*Alice's Adventures in Wonderland* by Lewis Carroll)

coming out VERB when a girl came out in society it meant she was of marriageable age. In order to 'come out' girls were expecting to attend balls and other parties during a season ❑ *The younger girls formed hopes of coming out a year or two sooner than they might otherwise have done* (*Pride and Prejudice* by Jane Austen)

commit VERB commit means arrest or stop ❑ *Commit the rascals* (*Doctor Faustus 4.7* by Christopher Marlowe)

commodious ADJ commodious means convenient ❑ *the most commodious and effectual ways* (*Gulliver's Travels* by Jonathan Swift)

commons NOUN commons is an old term meaning food shared with others ❑ *his pauper assistants ranged themselves behind him; the gruel was served out; and a long grace was said over the short commons.* (*Oliver Twist* by Charles Dickens)

complacency NOUN here complacency means a desire to please others. Today complacency means feeling pleased with oneself without good reason. ❑ *Twas thy power that raised the first complacency in me* (*The Prelude* by William Wordsworth)

complaisance NOUN complaisance was eagerness to please ❑ *we cannot wonder at his complaisance* (*Pride and Prejudice* by Jane Austen)

complaisant ADJ complaisant means polite ❑ *extremely cheerful and* *complaisant to their guest* (*Gulliver's Travels* by Jonathan Swift)

conning VERB conning means learning by heart ❑ *Or conning more* (*The Prelude* by William Wordsworth)

consequent NOUN consequence ❑ *as avarice is the necessary consequent of old age* (*Gulliver's Travels* by Jonathan Swift)

consorts NOUN concerts ❑ *The King, who delighted in music, had frequent consorts at Court* (*Gulliver's Travels* by Jonathan Swift)

conversible ADJ conversible meant easy to talk to, companionable ❑ *He can be a conversible companion* (*Pride and Prejudice* by Jane Austen)

copper NOUN a copper is a large pot than can be heated directly over a fire ❑ *He gazed in stupefied astonishment on the small rebel for some seconds, and then clung for support to the copper* (*Oliver Twist* by Charles Dickens)

copper-stick NOUN a copper-stick is the long piece of wood used to stir washing in the copper (or boiler) which was usually the biggest cooking pot in the house ❑ *It was Christmas Eve, and I had to stir the pudding for next day, with a copper-stick, from seven to eight by the Dutch clock* (*Great Expectations* by Charles Dickens)

counting-house NOUN a counting house is a place where accountants work ❑ *Once upon a time – of all the good days in the year, on Christmas Eve – old Scrooge sat busy in his countinghouse* (*A Christmas Carol* by Charles Dickens)

courtier NOUN a courtier is someone who attends the king or queen – a member of the court ❑ *next the ten courtiers;* (*Alice's Adventures in Wonderland* by Lewis Carroll)

covies NOUN covies were flocks of partridges ❑ *and will save all of the best covies for you* (*Pride and Prejudice* by Jane Austen)

cowed VERB cowed means frightened or intimidated ❑ *it cowed me more than the pain* (*Treasure Island* by Robert Louis Stevenson)

cozened VERB cozened means tricked or deceived ❑ *Do you remember, sir, how you cozened me* (*Doctor Faustus 4.7* by Christopher Marlowe)

cravats NOUN a cravat is a folded cloth that a man wears wrapped around his neck as a decorative item of clothing ❑ *we'd'a' slept in our cravats to-night* (*The Adventures of Huckleberry Finn* by Mark Twain)

crock and dirt phrase crock and dirt is an old expression meaning soot and dirt ❑ *and the mare catching cold at the door, and the boy grimed with crock and dirt* (*Great Expectations* by Charles Dickens)

crockery NOUN here crockery means pottery ❑ *By one of the parrots was a cat made of crockery* (*The Adventures of Huckleberry Finn* by Mark Twain)

crooked sixpence phrase it was considered unlucky to have a bent sixpence ❑ *You've got the beauty, you see, and I've got the luck, so you must keep me by you for your crooked sixpence* (*Silas Marner* by George Eliot)

croquet NOUN croquet is a traditional English summer game in which players try to hit wooden balls through hoops ❑ *and once she remembered trying to box her own ears for having cheated herself in a game of croquet* (*Alice's Adventures in Wonderland* by Lewis Carroll)

cross prep across ❑ *The two great streets, which run cross and divide it into four quarters* (Gulliver's Travels by Jonathan Swift)

culpable ADJ if you are culpable for something it means you are to blame ❑ *deep are the sorrows that spring from false ideas for which no man is culpable.* (*Silas Marner* by George Eliot)

cultured ADJ cultivated ❑ *Nor less when spring had warmed the cultured Vale* (*The Prelude* by William Wordsworth)

cupidity NOUN cupidity is greed ❑ *These people hated me with the hatred of cupidity and disappointment.* (*Great Expectations* by Charles Dickens)

curricle NOUN an open two-wheeled carriage with one seat for the driver and space for a single passenger ❑ *and they saw a lady and a gentleman in a curricle* (*Pride and Prejudice* by Jane Austen)

cynosure NOUN a cynosure is something that strongly attracts attention or admiration ❑ *Then I thought of Eliza and Georgiana; I beheld one the cynosure of a ballroom, the other the inmate of a convent cell* (*Jane Eyre* by Charlotte Brontë)

dalliance NOUN someone's dalliance with something is a brief involvement with it ❑ *nor sporting in the dalliance of love* (*Doctor Faustus Chorus* by Christopher Marlowe)

darkling ADV darkling is an archaic way of saying in the dark ❑ *Darkling I listen* (*Ode on a Nightingale* by John Keats)

delf-case NOUN a sideboard for holding dishes and crockery ❑ *at the pewter dishes and delf-case* (*Wuthering Heights* by Emily Brontë)

determined ◼ VERB here determined means ended ❑ *and be out of vogue when that was determined* (*Gulliver's Travels* by Jonathan Swift) ◼ VERB determined can mean to have been learned or found especially by investigation or experience ❑ *All the sensitive feelings it wounded so cruelly, all the shame and misery it kept alive within my breast, became more poignant as I thought of this; and I determined that the life was unendurable* (*David Copperfield* by Charles Dickens)

Deuce NOUN a slang term for the Devil ❑ *Ah, I dare say I did.*

Deuce take me, he added suddenly, I know I did. I find I am not quite unscrewed yet. (*Great Expectations* by Charles Dickens)

diabolical ADJ diabolical means devilish or evil ❑ *and with a thousand diabolical expressions* (*Treasure Island* by Robert Louis Stevenson)

direction NOUN here direction means address ❑ *Elizabeth was not surprised at it, as Jane had written the direction remarkably ill* (*Pride and Prejudice* by Jane Austen)

discover VERB to make known or announce ❑ *the Emperor would discover the secret while I was out of his power* (*Gulliver's Travels* by Jonathan Swift)

dissemble VERB hide or conceal ❑ *Dissemble nothing* (*On His Mistress* by John Donne)

dissolve VERB dissolve here means to release from life, to die ❑ *Fade far away, dissolve, and quite forget* (*Ode on a Nightingale* by John Keats)

distrain VERB to distrain is to seize the property of someone who is in debt in compensation for the money owed ❑ *for he's threatening to distrain for it* (*Silas Marner* by George Eliot)

Divan NOUN a Divan was originally a Turkish council of state – the name was transferred to the couches they sat on and is used to mean this in English ❑ *Mr Brass applauded this picture very much, and the bed being soft and comfortable, Mr Quilp determined to use it, both as a sleeping place by night and as a kind of Divan by day.* (*The Old Curiosity Shop* by Charles Dickens)

divorcement NOUN separation ❑ *By all pains which want and divorcement hath* (*On His Mistress* by John Donne)

dog in the manger, a phrase this phrase describes someone who prevents you from enjoying something that they themselves have no need for ❏ *You are a dog in the manger, Cathy, and desire no one to be loved but yourself* (*Wuthering Heights* by Emily Brontë)

dolorifuge NOUN dolorifuge is a word which Thomas Hardy invented. It means pain-killer or comfort ❏ *as a species of dolorifuge* (*Tess of the D'Urbervilles* by Thomas Hardy)

dome NOUN building ❏ *that river and that mouldering dome* (*The Prelude* by William Wordsworth)

domestic phrase here domestic means a person's management of the house ❏ *to give some account of my domestic* (*Gulliver's Travels* by Jonathan Swift)

dunce NOUN a dunce is another word for idiot ❏ *Do you take me for a dunce? Go on?* (*Alice's Adventures in Wonderland* by Lewis Carroll)

Ecod exclam a slang exclamation meaning 'oh God!' ❏ *"Ecod,"* replied Wemmick, shaking his head, *"that's not my trade."* (*Great Expectations* by Charles Dickens)

egg-hot NOUN an egg-hot (see also 'flip' and 'negus') was a hot drink made from beer and eggs, sweetened with nutmeg ❏ *She fainted when she saw me return, and made a little jug of egg-hot afterwards to console us while we talked it over.* (*David Copperfield* by Charles Dickens)

encores NOUN an encore is a short extra performance at the end of a longer one, which the entertainer gives because the audience has enthusiastically asked for it ❏ *we want a little something to answer encores with, anyway* (*The Adventures of Huckleberry Finn* by Mark Twain)

equipage NOUN an elegant and impressive carriage ❏ *and besides, the equipage did not answer to any of their neighbours* (*Pride and Prejudice* by Jane Austen)

exordium NOUN an exordium is the opening part of a speech ❏ *"Now, Handel,"* as if it were the grave beginning of a portentous business exordium, he had suddenly given up that tone (*Great Expectations* by Charles Dickens)

expect VERB here expect means to wait for ❏ *to expect his farther commands* (*Gulliver's Travels* by Jonathan Swift)

familiars NOUN familiars means spirits or devils who come to someone when they are called ❏ *I'll turn all the lice about thee into familiars* (*Doctor Faustus* 1.4 by Christopher Marlowe)

fantods NOUN a fantod is a person who fidgets or can't stop moving nervously ❏ *It most give me the fantods* (*The Adventures of Huckleberry Finn* by Mark Twain)

farthing NOUN a farthing is an old unit of British currency which was worth a quarter of a penny ❏ *Not a farthing less. A great many back-payments are included in it, I assure you.* (*A Christmas Carol* by Charles Dickens)

farthingale NOUN a hoop worn under a skirt to extend it ❏ *A bell with an old voice – which I dare say in its time had often said to the house, Here is the green farthingale* (*Great Expectations* by Charles Dickens)

favours NOUN here favours is an old word which means ribbons ❏ *A group of humble mourners entered the gate: wearing white favours* (*Oliver Twist* by Charles Dickens)

feigned VERB pretend or pretending ❏ *not my feigned page* (*On His Mistress* by John Donne)

fence 1 NOUN a fence is someone who receives and sells stolen goods ❏ *What are you up to? Ill-treating the boys, you covetous, avaricious, in-sa-ti-a-ble old fence?* (*Oliver Twist* by Charles Dickens) 2 NOUN defence or protection ❏ *but honesty hath no fence against superior cunning* (*Gulliver's Travels* by Jonathan Swift)

fess ADJ fess is an old word which means pleased or proud ❏ *You'll be* *fess enough, my poppet* (*Tess of the D'Urbervilles* by Thomas Hardy)

fettered ADJ fettered means bound in chains or chained ❑ *"You are fettered," said Scrooge, trembling. "Tell me why?"* (*A Christmas Carol* by Charles Dickens)

fidges VERB fidges means fidgets, which is to keep moving your hands slightly because you are nervous or excited ❑ *Look, Jim, how my fingers fidges* (*Treasure Island* by Robert Louis Stevenson)

finger-post NOUN a finger-post is a sign-post showing the direction to different places ❑ *"The gallows," continued Fagin, "the gallows, my dear, is an ugly finger-post, which points out a very short and sharp turning that has stopped many a bold fellow's career on the broad highway."* (*Oliver Twist* by Charles Dickens)

fire-irons NOUN fire-irons are tools kept by the side of the fire to either cook with or look after the fire ❑ *the fire-irons came first* (*Alice's Adventures in Wonderland* by Lewis Carroll)

fire-plug NOUN a fire-plug is another word for a fire hydrant ❑ *The pony looked with great attention into a fire-plug, which was near him, and appeared to be quite absorbed in contemplating it* (*The Old Curiosity Shop* by Charles Dickens)

flank NOUN flank is the side of an animal ❑ *And all her silken flanks with garlands dressed* (*Ode on a Grecian Urn* by John Keats)

flip NOUN a flip is a drink made from warmed ale, sugar, spice and beaten egg ❑ *The events of the day, in combination with the twins, if not with the flip, had made Mrs. Micawber hysterical, and she shed tears as she replied* (*David Copperfield* by Charles Dickens)

flit VERB flit means to move quickly ❑ *and if he had meant to flit to Thrushcross Grange* (*Wuthering Heights* by Emily Brontë)

floorcloth NOUN a floorcloth was a hard-wearing piece of canvas used instead of carpet ❑ *This avenging phantom was ordered to be on duty at eight on Tuesday morning in the hall (it was two feet square, as charged for floorcloth)* (*Great Expectations* by Charles Dickens)

fly-driver NOUN a fly-driver is a carriage drawn by a single horse ❑ *The fly-drivers, among whom I inquired next, were equally jocose and equally disrespectful* (*David Copperfield* by Charles Dickens)

fob NOUN a small pocket in which a watch is kept ❑ *"Certain," replied the man, drawing a gold watch from his fob* (*Oliver Twist* by Charles Dickens)

folly NOUN folly means foolishness or stupidity ❑ *the folly of beginning a work* (*Robinson Crusoe* by Daniel Defoe)

fond ADJ fond means foolish ❑ *Fond worldling* (*Doctor Faustus 5.2* by Christopher Marlowe)

fondness NOUN silly or foolish affection ❑ *They have no fondness for their colts or foals* (*Gulliver's Travels* by Jonathan Swift)

for his fancy phrase for his fancy means for his liking or as he wanted ❑ *and as I did not obey quick enough for his fancy* (*Treasure Island* by Robert Louis Stevenson)

forlorn ADJ lost or very upset ❑ *you are from that day forlorn* (*Gulliver's Travels* by Jonathan Swift)

foster-sister NOUN a foster-sister was someone brought up by the same nurse or in the same household ❑ *I had been his foster-sister* (*Wuthering Heights* by Emily Brontë)

fox-fire NOUN fox-fire is a weak glow that is given off by decaying, rotten wood ❑ *what we must have was a lot of them rotten chunks that's called fox-fire* (*The Adventures of Huckleberry Finn* by Mark Twain)

frozen sea phrase the Arctic Ocean ❑ *into the frozen sea* (*Gulliver's Travels* by Jonathan Swift)

gainsay VERB to gainsay something is to say it isn't true or to deny it ❑ *"So she had," cried Scrooge. "You're right. I'll not gainsay it, Spirit. God forbid!" (A Christmas Carol* by Charles Dickens)

gaiters NOUN gaiters were leggings made of a cloth or piece of leather which covered the leg from the knee to the ankle ❑ *Mr Knightley was hard at work upon the lower buttons of his thick leather gaiters (Emma* by Jane Austen)

galluses NOUN galluses is an old spelling of gallows, and here means suspenders. Suspenders are straps worn over someone's shoulders and fastened to their trousers to prevent the trousers falling down ❑ *and home-knit galluses (The Adventures of Huckleberry Finn* by Mark Twain)

galoot NOUN a sailor but also a clumsy person ❑ *and maybe a galoot on it chopping (The Adventures of Huckleberry Finn* by Mark Twain)

gayest ADJ gayest means the most lively and bright or merry ❑ *Beth played her gayest march (Little Women* by Louisa May Alcott)

gem NOUN here gem means jewellery ❑ *the mountain shook off turf and flower, had only heath for raiment and crag for gem (Jane Eyre* by Charlotte Brontë)

giddy ADJ giddy means dizzy ❑ *and I wish you wouldn't keep appearing and vanishing so suddenly; you make one quite giddy. (Alice's Adventures in Wonderland* by Lewis Carroll)

gig NOUN a light two-wheeled carriage ❑ *when a gig drove up to the garden gate: out of which there jumped a fat gentleman (Oliver Twist* by Charles Dickens)

gladsome ADJ gladsome is an old word meaning glad or happy ❑ *Nobody ever stopped him in the street to say, with gladsome looks (A Christmas Carol* by Charles Dickens)

glen NOUN a glen is a small valley; the word is used commonly in Scotland ❑ *a beck which follows the bend of the glen (Wuthering Heights* by Emily Brontë)

gravelled VERB gravelled is an old term which means to baffle or defeat someone ❑ *Gravelled the pastors of the German Church (Doctor Faustus 1.1* by Christopher Marlowe)

grinder NOUN a grinder was a private tutor ❑ *but that when he had had the happiness of marrying Mrs Pocket very early in his life, he had impaired his prospects and taken up the calling of a Grinder (Great Expectations* by Charles Dickens)

gruel NOUN gruel is a thin, watery cornmeal or oatmeal soup ❑ *and the little saucepan of gruel (Scrooge had a cold in his head) upon the hob. (A Christmas Carol* by Charles Dickens)

guinea, half a NOUN a half guinea was ten shillings and sixpence ❑ *but lay out half a guinea at Ford's (Emma* by Jane Austen)

gull VERB gull is an old term which means to fool or deceive someone ❑ *Hush, I'll gull him supernaturally (Doctor Faustus 3.4* by Christopher Marlowe)

gunnel NOUN the gunnel, or gunwhale, is the upper edge of a boat's side ❑ *But he put his foot on the gunnel and rocked her (The Adventures of Huckleberry Finn* by Mark Twain)

gunwale NOUN the side of a ship ❑ *He dipped his hand in the water over the boat's gunwale (Great Expectations* by Charles Dickens)

Gytrash NOUN a Gytrash is an omen of misfortune to the superstitious, usually taking the form of a hound ❑ *I remembered certain of Bessie's tales, wherein figured a North-of-England spirit, called a 'Gytrash' (Jane Eyre* by Charlotte Brontë)

hackney-cabriolet NOUN a two-wheeled carriage with four seats for hire and pulled by a horse ❑ *A hackney-cabriolet was in waiting; with the same vehemence which she had exhibited in addressing Oliver, the girl pulled him in with her, and drew the curtains close.* (*Oliver Twist* by Charles Dickens)

hackney-coach NOUN a four-wheeled horse-drawn vehicle for hire ❑ *The twilight was beginning to close in, when Mr. Brownlow alighted from a hackney-coach at his own door, and knocked softly.* (*Oliver Twist* by Charles Dickens)

haggler NOUN a haggler is someone who travels from place to place selling small goods and items ❑ *when I be plain Jack Durbeyfield, the haggler* (*Tess of the D'Urbervilles* by Thomas Hardy)

halter NOUN a halter is a rope or strap used to lead an animal or to tie it up ❑ *I had of course long been used to a halter and a headstall* (*Black Beauty* by Anna Sewell)

hamlet NOUN a hamlet is a small village or a group of houses in the countryside ❑ *down from the hamlet* (*Treasure Island* by Robert Louis Stevenson)

hand-barrow NOUN a hand-barrow is a device for carrying heavy objects. It is like a wheelbarrow except that it has handles, rather than wheels, for moving the barrow ❑ *his sea chest following behind him in a hand-barrow* (*Treasure Island* by Robert Louis Stevenson)

handspike NOUN a handspike was a stick which was used as a lever ❑ *a bit of stick like a handspike* (*Treasure Island* by Robert Louis Stevenson)

haply ADV haply means by chance or perhaps ❑ *And haply the Queen-Moon is on her throne* (*Ode on a Nightingale* by John Keats)

harem NOUN the harem was the part of the house where the women lived ❑ *mostly they hang round the harem* (*The Adventures of Huckleberry Finn* by Mark Twain)

hautboys NOUN hautboys are oboes ❑ *sausages and puddings resembling flutes and hautboys* (*Gulliver's Travels* by Jonathan Swift)

hawker NOUN a hawker is someone who sells goods to people as he travels rather than from a fixed place like a shop ❑ *to buy some stockings from a hawker* (*Treasure Island* by Robert Louis Stevenson)

hawser NOUN a hawser is a rope used to tie up or tow a ship or boat ❑ *Again among the tiers of shipping, in and out, avoiding rusty chain-cables, frayed hempen hawsers* (*Great Expectations* by Charles Dickens)

headstall NOUN the headstall is the part of the bridle or halter that goes around a horse's head ❑ *I had of course long been used to a halter and a headstall* (*Black Beauty* by Anna Sewell)

hearken VERB hearken means to listen ❑ *though we sometimes stopped to lay hold of each other and hearken* (*Treasure Island* by Robert Louis Stevenson)

heartless ADJ here heartless means without heart or dejected ❑ *I am not heartless* (*The Prelude* by William Wordsworth)

hebdomadal ADJ hebdomadal means weekly ❑ *It was the hebdomadal treat to which we all looked forward from Sabbath to Sabbath* (*Jane Eyre* by Charlotte Brontë)

highwaymen NOUN highwaymen were people who stopped travellers and robbed them ❑ *We are highwaymen* (*The Adventures of Huckleberry Finn* by Mark Twain)

hinds NOUN hinds means farm hands, or people who work on a farm ❑ *He called his hinds about him* (*Gulliver's Travels* by Jonathan Swift)

histrionic ADJ if you refer to someone's behaviour as histrionic, you are being critical of it because it is dramatic and exaggerated

❏ *But the histrionic muse is the darling* (*The Adventures of Huckleberry Finn* by Mark Twain)

hogs NOUN hogs is another word for pigs ❏ *Tom called the hogs 'ingots'* (*The Adventures of Huckleberry Finn* by Mark Twain)

horrors NOUN the horrors are a fit, called delirium tremens, which is caused by drinking too much alcohol ❏ *I'll have the horrors* (*Treasure Island* by Robert Louis Stevenson)

huffy ADJ huffy means to be obviously annoyed or offended about something ❏ *They will feel that more than angry speeches or huffy actions* (*Little Women* by Louisa May Alcott)

hulks NOUN hulks were prison-ships ❏ *The miserable companion of thieves and ruffians, the fallen outcast of low haunts, the associate of the scourings of the jails and hulks* (*Oliver Twist* by Charles Dickens)

humbug NOUN humbug means nonsense or rubbish ❏ *"Bah," said Scrooge. "Humbug!"* (*A Christmas Carol* by Charles Dickens)

humours NOUN it was believed that there were four fluids in the body called humours which decided the temperament of a person depending on how much of each fluid was present ❏ *other peccant humours* (*Gulliver's Travels* by Jonathan Swift)

husbandry NOUN husbandry is farming animals ❏ *bad husbandry were plentifully anointing their wheels* (*Silas Marner* by George Eliot)

huswife NOUN a huswife was a small sewing kit ❏ *but I had put my huswife on it* (*Emma* by Jane Austen)

ideal ADJ ideal in this context means imaginary ❏ *I discovered the yell was not ideal* (*Wuthering Heights* by Emily Brontë)

If our two phrase if both our ❏ *If our two loves be one* (*The Good-Morrow* by John Donne)

ignis-fatuus NOUN ignis-fatuus is the light given out by burning marsh gases, which lead careless travellers into danger ❏ *it is madness in all women to let a secret love kindle within them, which, if unreturned and unknown, must devour the life that feeds it; and, if discovered and responded to, must lead ignis-fatuus-like, into miry wilds whence there is no extrication.* (*Jane Eyre* by Charlotte Brontë)

imaginations NOUN here imaginations means schemes or plans ❏ *soon drove out those imaginations* (*Gulliver's Travels* by Jonathan Swift)

impressible ADJ impressible means open or impressionable ❏ *for Marner had one of those impressible, self-doubting natures* (*Silas Marner* by George Eliot)

in good intelligence phrase friendly with each other ❏ *that these two persons were in good intelligence with each other* (*Gulliver's Travels* by Jonathan Swift)

inanity NOUN inanity is sillyness or dull stupidity ❏ *Do we not wile away moments of inanity* (*Silas Marner* by George Eliot)

incivility NOUN incivility means rudeness or impoliteness ❏ *if it's only for a piece of incivility like to-night's* (*Treasure Island* by Robert Louis Stevenson)

indigenae NOUN indigenae means natives or people from that area ❏ *an exotic that the surly indigenae will not recognise for kin* (*Wuthering Heights* by Emily Brontë)

indocible ADJ unteachable ❏ *so they were the most restive and indocible* (*Gulliver's Travels* by Jonathan Swift)

ingenuity NOUN inventiveness ❏ *entreated me to give him something as an encouragement to ingenuity* (*Gulliver's Travels* by Jonathan Swift)

ingots NOUN an ingot is a lump of a valuable metal like gold, usually shaped like a brick ❑ *Tom called the hogs 'ingots'* (*The Adventures of Huckleberry Finn* by Mark Twain)

inkstand NOUN an inkstand is a pot which was put on a desk to contain either ink or pencils and pens ❑ *throwing an inkstand at the Lizard as she spoke* (*Alice's Adventures in Wonderland* by Lewis Carroll)

inordinate ADJ without order. Today inordinate means 'excessive'. ❑ *Though yet untutored and inordinate* (*The Prelude* by William Wordsworth)

intellectuals NOUN here intellectuals means the minds (of the workmen) ❑ *those instructions they give being too refined for the intellectuals of their workmen* (*Gulliver's Travels* by Jonathan Swift)

interview NOUN meeting ❑ *By our first strange and fatal interview* (*On His Mistress* by John Donne)

jacks NOUN jacks are rods for turning a spit over a fire ❑ *It was a small bit of pork suspended from the kettle hanger by a string passed through a large door key, in a way known to primitive housekeepers unpossessed of jacks* (*Silas Marner* by George Eliot)

jews-harp NOUN a jews-harp is a small, metal, musical instrument that is played by the mouth ❑ *A jews-harp's plenty good enough for a rat* (*The Adventures of Huckleberry Finn* by Mark Twain)

jorum NOUN a large bowl ❑ *while Miss Skiffins brewed such a jorum of tea, that the pig in the back premises became strongly excited* (*Great Expectations* by Charles Dickens)

jostled VERB jostled means bumped or pushed by someone or some people ❑ *being jostled himself into the kennel* (*Gulliver's Travels* by Jonathan Swift)

keepsake NOUN a keepsake is a gift which reminds someone of an event or of the person who gave it to them. ❑ *books and ornaments they had in their boudoirs at home: keepsakes that different relations had presented to them* (*Jane Eyre* by Charlotte Brontë)

kenned VERB kenned means knew ❑ *though little kenned the lamplighter that he had any company but Christmas!* (*A Christmas Carol* by Charles Dickens)

kennel NOUN kennel means gutter, which is the edge of a road next to the pavement, where rain water collects and flows away ❑ *being jostled himself into the kennel* (*Gulliver's Travels* by Jonathan Swift)

knock-knee ADJ knock-knee means slanted, at an angle. ❑ *LOT 1 was marked in whitewashed knock-knee letters on the pavement* (*Great Expectations* by Charles Dickens)

ladylike ADJ to be ladylike is to behave in a polite, dignified and graceful way ❑ *No, winking isn't ladylike* (*Little Women* by Louisa May Alcott)

lapse NOUN flow ❑ *Stealing with silent lapse to join the brook* (*The Prelude* by William Wordsworth)

larry NOUN larry is an old word which means commotion or noisy celebration ❑ *That was all a part of the larry!* (*Tess of the D'Urbervilles* by Thomas Hardy)

laths NOUN laths are strips of wood ❑ *The panels shrunk, the windows cracked; fragments of plaster fell out of the ceiling, and the naked laths were shown instead* (A Christmas Carol by Charles Dickens)

leer NOUN a leer is an unpleasant smile ❑ *with a kind of leer* (*Treasure Island* by Robert Louis Stevenson)

lenitives NOUN these are different kinds of drugs or medicines: lenitives and palliatives were pain relievers; aperitives were laxatives; abstersives caused vomiting; corrosives destroyed human tissue; restringents caused constipation; cephalalgics stopped headaches;

icterics were used as medicine for jaundice; apophlegmatics were cough medicine, and acoustics were cures for the loss of hearing ❏ *lenitives, aperitives, abstersives, corrosives, restringents, palliatives, laxatives, cephalalgics, icterics, apophlegmatics, acoustics* (*Gulliver's Travels* by Jonathan Swift)

lest CONJ in case. If you do something lest something (usually) unpleasant happens you do it to try to prevent it happening ❏ *She went in without knocking, and hurried upstairs, in great fear lest she should meet the real Mary Ann* (*Alice's Adventures in Wonderland* by Lewis Carroll)

levee NOUN a levee is an old term for a meeting held in the morning, shortly after the person holding the meeting has got out of bed ❏ *I used to attend the King's levee once or twice a week* (*Gulliver's Travels* by Jonathan Swift)

life-preserver NOUN a club which had lead inside it to make it heavier and therefore more dangerous ❏ *and with no more suspicious articles displayed to view than two or three heavy bludgeons which stood in a corner, and a 'life-preserver' that hung over the chimney-piece.* (*Oliver Twist* by Charles Dickens)

lighterman NOUN a lighterman is another word for sailor ❏ *in and out, hammers going in ship-builders' yards, saws going at timber, clashing engines going at things unknown, pumps going in leaky ships, capstans going, ships going out to sea, and unintelligible sea creatures roaring curses over the bulwarks at respondent lightermen* (*Great Expectations* by Charles Dickens)

livery NOUN servants often wore a uniform known as a livery ❏ *suddenly a footman in livery came running out of the wood* (*Alice's Adventures in Wonderland* by Lewis Carroll)

livid ADJ livid means pale or ash coloured. Livid also means very angry ❏ *a dirty, livid white*

(*Treasure Island* by Robert Louis Stevenson)

lottery-tickets NOUN a popular card game ❏ *and Mrs. Philips protested that they would have a nice comfortable noisy game of lottery tickets* (*Pride and Prejudice* by Jane Austen)

lower and upper world phrase the earth and the heavens are the lower and upper worlds ❏ *the changes in the lower and upper world* (*Gulliver's Travels* by Jonathan Swift)

lustres NOUN lustres are chandeliers. A chandelier is a large, decorative frame which holds light bulbs or candles and hangs from the ceiling ❏ *the lustres, lights, the carving and the guilding* (*The Prelude* by William Wordsworth)

lynched VERB killed without a criminal trial by a crowd of people ❏ *He'll never know how nigh he come to getting lynched* (*The Adventures of Huckleberry Finn* by Mark Twain)

malingering VERB if someone is malingering they are pretending to be ill to avoid working ❏ *And you stand there malingering* (*Treasure Island* by Robert Louis Stevenson)

managing phrase treating with consideration ❏ *to think the honour of my own kind not worth managing* (*Gulliver's Travels* by Jonathan Swift)

manhood phrase manhood means human nature ❏ *concerning the nature of manhood* (*Gulliver's Travels* by Jonathan Swift)

man-trap NOUN a man-trap is a set of steel jaws that snap shut when trodden on and trap a person's leg ❏ *"Don't go to him," I called out of the window, "he's an assassin! A man-trap!"* (*Oliver Twist* by Charles Dickens)

maps NOUN charts of the night sky ❏ *Let maps to others, worlds on worlds have shown* (*The Good-Morrow* by John Donne)

mark VERB look at or notice ❑ Mark but this flea, and mark in this (The Flea by John Donne)

maroons NOUN A maroon is someone who has been left in a place which it is difficult for them to escape from, like a small island ❑ if schooners, islands, and maroons (Treasure Island by Robert Louis Stevenson)

mast NOUN here mast means the fruit of forest trees ❑ a quantity of acorns, dates, chestnuts, and other mast (Gulliver's Travels by Jonathan Swift)

mate VERB defeat ❑ Where Mars did mate the warlike Carthigens (Doctor Faustus Chorus by Christopher Marlowe)

mealy ADJ Mealy when used to describe a face meant palid, pale or colourless ❑ I only know two sorts of boys. Mealy boys, and beef-faced boys (Oliver Twist by Charles Dickens)

middling ADJ fairly or moderately ❑ she worked me middling hard for about an hour (The Adventures of Huckleberry Finn by Mark Twain)

mill NOUN a mill, or treadmill, was a device for hard labour or punishment in prison ❑ Was you never on the mill? (Oliver Twist by Charles Dickens)

milliner's shop NOUN a milliner's sold fabrics, clothing, lace and accessories; as time went on they specialized more and more in hats ❑ to pay their duty to their aunt and to a milliner's shop just over the way (Pride and Prejudice by Jane Austen)

minching un' munching phrase how people in the north of England used to describe the way people from the south speak ❑ Minching un' munching! (Wuthering Heights by Emily Brontë)

mine NOUN gold ❑ Whether both th'Indias of spice and mine (The Sun Rising by John Donne)

mire NOUN mud ❑ Tis my fate to be always ground into the mire under the iron heel of oppression (The Adventures of Huckleberry Finn by Mark Twain)

miscellany NOUN a miscellany is a collection of many different kinds of things ❑ under that, the miscellany began (Treasure Island by Robert Louis Stevenson)

mistarshers NOUN mistarshers means moustache, which is the hair that grows on a man's upper lip ❑ when he put his hand up to his mistarshers (Tess of the D'Urbervilles by Thomas Hardy)

morrow NOUN here good-morrow means tomorrow and a new and better life ❑ And now good-morrow to our waking souls (The Good-Morrow by John Donne)

mortification NOUN mortification is an old word for gangrene which is when part of the body decays or 'dies' because of disease ❑ Yes, it was a mortification – that was it (The Adventures of Huckleberry Finn by Mark Twain)

mought PARTICIPLE mought is an old spelling of might ❑ what you mought call me? You mought call me captain (Treasure Island by Robert Louis Stevenson)

move VERB move me not means do not make me angry ❑ Move me not, Faustus (Doctor Faustus 2.1 by Christopher Marlowe)

muffin-cap NOUN a muffin cap is a flat cap made from wool ❑ the old one, remained stationary in the muffin-cap and leathers (Oliver Twist by Charles Dickens)

mulatter NOUN a mulatter was another word for mulatto, which is a person with parents who are from different races ❑ a mulatter, most as white as a white man (The Adventures of Huckleberry Finn by Mark Twain)

mummery NOUN mummery is an old word that meant meaningless (or pretentious) ceremony ❑ When they were all gone, and when Trabb and his men – but not his boy: I looked for him – had crammed *their mummery into bags, and were gone too, the house felt wholesomer.* (*Great Expectations* by Charles Dickens)

nap NOUN the nap is the woolly surface on a new item of clothing. Here the surface has been worn away so it looks bare ❑ *like an old hat with the nap rubbed off* (*The Adventures of Huckleberry Finn* by Mark Twain)

natural **1** NOUN a natural is a person born with learning difficulties ❑ *though he had been left to his particular care by their deceased father, who thought him almost a natural.* (*David Copperfield* by Charles Dickens) **2** ADJ natural meant illegitimate ❑ *Harriet Smith was the natural daughter of somebody* (*Emma* by Jane Austen)

navigator NOUN a navigator was originally someone employed to dig canals. It is the origin of the word 'navvy' meaning a labourer ❑ *She ascertained from me in a few words what it was all about, comforted Dora, and gradually convinced her that I was not a labourer – from my manner of stating the case I believe Dora concluded that I was a navigator, and went balancing myself up and down a plank all day with a wheelbarrow – and so brought us together in peace.* (*David Copperfield* by Charles Dickens)

necromancy NOUN necromancy means a kind of magic where the magician speaks to spirits or ghosts to find out what will happen in the future ❑ *He surfeits upon cursed necromancy* (*Doctor Faustus chorus* by Christopher Marlowe)

negus NOUN a negus is a hot drink made from sweetened wine and water ❑ *He sat placidly perusing the newspaper, with his little head on one side, and a glass of warm sherry negus at his elbow.* (*David Copperfield* by Charles Dickens)

nice ADJ discriminating. Able to make good judgements or choices ❑

consequently a claim to be nice (*Emma* by Jane Austen)

nigh ADV nigh means near ❑ *He'll never know how nigh he come to getting lynched* (*The Adventures of Huckleberry Finn* by Mark Twain)

nimbleness NOUN nimbleness means being able to move very quickly or skillfully ❑ *and with incredible accuracy and nimbleness* (*Treasure Island* by Robert Louis Stevenson)

noggin NOUN a noggin is a small mug or a wooden cup ❑ *you'll bring me one noggin of rum* (*Treasure Island* by Robert Louis Stevenson)

none ADJ neither ❑ *none can die* (*The Good-Morrow* by John Donne)

notices NOUN observations ❑ *Arch are his notices* (*The Prelude* by William Wordsworth)

occiput NOUN occiput means the back of the head ❑ *saw off the occiput of each couple* (*Gulliver's Travels* by Jonathan Swift)

officiously ADJ kindly ❑ *the governess who attended Glumdalclitch very officiously lifted me up* (*Gulliver's Travels* by Jonathan Swift)

old salt phrase old salt is a slang term for an experienced sailor ❑ *a 'true sea-dog', and a 'real old salt'* (*Treasure Island* by Robert Louis Stevenson)

or ere phrase before ❑ *or ere the Hall was built* (*The Prelude* by William Wordsworth)

ostler NOUN one who looks after horses at an inn ❑ *The bill paid, and the waiter remembered, and the ostler not forgotten, and the chambermaid taken into consideration* (*Great Expectations* by Charles Dickens)

ostry NOUN an ostry is an old word for a pub or hotel ❑ *lest I send you into the ostry with a vengeance* (*Doctor Faustus 2.2* by Christopher Marlowe)

outrunning the constable phrase outrunning the constable meant spending more than you earn ❑ *but I shall by this means be able to* *check your bills and to pull you up if I find you outrunning the constable.* (*Great Expectations* by Charles Dickens)

over ADJ across ❑ *It is in length six yards, and in the thickest part at least three yards over* (*Gulliver's Travels* by Jonathan Swift)

over the broomstick phrase this is a phrase meaning 'getting married without a formal ceremony' ❑ *They both led tramping lives, and this woman in Gerrard-street here, had been married very young, over the broomstick (as we say), to a tramping man, and was a perfect fury in point of jealousy.* (*Great Expectations* by Charles Dickens)

own VERB own means to admit or to acknowledge ❑ *It's my old girl that advises. She has the head. But I never own to it before her. Discipline must be maintained* (*Bleak House* by Charles Dickens)

page NOUN here page means a boy employed to run errands ❑ *not my feigned page* (*On His Mistress* by John Donne)

paid pretty dear phrase paid pretty dear means paid a high price or suffered quite a lot ❑ *I paid pretty dear for my monthly fourpenny piece* (*Treasure Island* by Robert Louis Stevenson)

pannikins NOUN pannikins were small tin cups ❑ *of lifting light glasses and cups to his lips, as if they were clumsy pannikins* (*Great Expectations* by Charles Dickens)

pards NOUN pards are leopards ❑ *Not charioted by Bacchus and his pards* (*Ode on a Nightingale* by John Keats)

parlour boarder NOUN a pupil who lived with the family ❑ *and somebody had lately raised her from the condition of scholar to parlour boarder* (*Emma* by Jane Austen)

particular, a London phrase London in Victorian times and up to the 1950s was famous for having very dense fog – which was a combination of real fog and the

smog of pollution from factories ❑ *This is a London particular . . . A fog, miss'* (*Bleak House* by Charles Dickens)

patten NOUN pattens were wooden soles which were fixed to shoes by straps to protect the shoes in wet weather ❑ *carrying a basket like the Great Seal of England in plaited straw, a pair of pattens, a spare shawl, and an umbrella, though it was a fine bright day* (*Great Expectations* by Charles Dickens)

paviour NOUN a paviour was a labourer who worked on the street pavement ❑ *the paviour his pickaxe* (*Oliver Twist* by Charles Dickens)

peccant ADJ peccant means unhealthy ❑ *other peccant humours* (*Gulliver's Travels* by Jonathan Swift)

penetralium NOUN penetralium is a word used to describe the inner rooms of the house ❑ *and I had no desire to aggravate his impatience previous to inspecting the penetralium* (*Wuthering Heights* by Emily Brontë)

pensive ADV pensive means deep in thought or thinking seriously about something ❑ *and she was leaning pensive on a tomb-stone on her right elbow* (*The Adventures of Huckleberry Finn* by Mark Twain)

penury NOUN penury is the state of being extremely poor ❑ *Distress, if not penury, loomed in the distance* (*Tess of the D'Urbervilles* by Thomas Hardy)

perspective NOUN telescope ❑ *a pocket perspective* (*Gulliver's Travels* by Jonathan Swift)

phaeton NOUN a phaeton was an open carriage for four people ❑ *often condescends to drive by my humble abode in her little phaeton and ponies* (*Pride and Prejudice* by Jane Austen)

phantasm NOUN a phantasm is an illusion, something that is not real. It is sometimes used to mean ghost ❑ *Experience had bred no fancies in* *him that could raise the phantasm of appetite* (*Silas Marner* by George Eliot)

physic NOUN here physic means medicine ❏ *there I studied physic two years and seven months* (*Gulliver's Travels* by Jonathan Swift)

pinioned VERB to pinion is to hold both arms so that a person cannot move them ❏ *But the relentless Ghost pinioned him in both his arms, and forced him to observe what happened next.* (*A Christmas Carol* by Charles Dickens)

piquet NOUN piquet was a popular card game in the C18th ❏ *Mr Hurst and Mr Bingley were at piquet* (*Pride and Prejudice* by Jane Austen)

plaister NOUN a plaister is a piece of cloth on which an apothecary (or pharmacist) would spread ointment. The cloth is then applied to wounds or bruises to treat them ❏ *Then, she gave the knife a final smart wipe on the edge of the plaister, and then sawed a very thick round off the loaf: which she finally, before separating from the loaf, hewed into two halves, of which Joe got one, and I the other.* (*Great Expectations* by Charles Dickens)

plantations NOUN here plantations means colonies, which are countries controlled by a more powerful country ❏ *besides our plantations in America* (*Gulliver's Travels* by Jonathan Swift)

plastic ADV here plastic is an old term meaning shaping or a power that was forming ❏ *A plastic power abode with me* (*The Prelude* by William Wordsworth)

players NOUN actors ❏ *of players which upon the world's stage be* (*On His Mistress* by John Donne)

plump ADV all at once, suddenly ❏ *But it took a bit of time to get it well round, the change come so uncommon plump, didn't it?* (*Great Expectations* by Charles Dickens)

plundered VERB to plunder is to rob or steal from ❏ *These crosses stand for the names of ships or towns that they sank or plundered* (*Treasure Island* by Robert Louis Stevenson)

pommel ■ VERB to pommel someone is to hit them repeatedly with your fists ❏ *hug him round the neck, pommel his back, and kick his legs in irrepressible affection!* (*A Christmas Carol* by Charles Dickens) ② NOUN a pommel is the part of a saddle that rises up at the front ❏ *He had his gun across his pommel* (*The Adventures of Huckleberry Finn* by Mark Twain)

poor's rates NOUN poor's rates were property taxes which were used to support the poor ❏ *"Oh!" replied the undertaker; "why, you know, Mr. Bumble, I pay a good deal towards the poor's rates."* (*Oliver Twist* by Charles Dickens)

popular ADJ popular means ruled by the people, or Republican, rather than ruled by a monarch ❏ *With those of Greece compared and popular Rome* (*The Prelude* by William Wordsworth)

porringer NOUN a porringer is a small bowl ❏ *Of this festive composition each boy had one porringer, and no more* (*Oliver Twist* by Charles Dickens)

postboy NOUN a postboy was the driver of a horse-drawn carriage ❏ *He spoke to a postboy who was dozing under the gateway* (*Oliver Twist* by Charles Dickens)

post-chaise NOUN a fast carriage for two or four passengers ❏ *Looking round, he saw that it was a post-chaise, driven at great speed* (*Oliver Twist* by Charles Dickens)

postern NOUN a small gate usually at the back of a building ❏ *The little servant happening to be entering the fortress with two hot rolls, I passed through the postern and crossed the drawbridge, in her company* (*Great Expectations* by Charles Dickens)

pottle NOUN a pottle was a small basket ❏ *He had a paper-bag under each arm and a pottle of* strawberries in one hand . . . (*Great Expectations* by Charles Dickens)

pounce NOUN pounce is a fine powder used to prevent ink spreading on untreated paper ❑ *in that grim atmosphere of pounce and parchment, red-tape, dusty wafers, ink-jars, brief and draft paper, law reports, writs, declarations, and bills of costs* (*David Copperfield* by Charles Dickens)

pox NOUN pox means sexually transmitted diseases like syphilis ❑ *how the pox in all its consequences and denominations* (*Gulliver's Travels* by Jonathan Swift)

prelibation NOUN prelibation means a foretaste of or an example of something to come ❑ *A prelibation to the mower's scythe* (*The Prelude* by William Wordsworth)

prentice NOUN an apprentice ❑ *and Joe, sitting on an old gun, had told me that when I was 'prentice to him regularly bound, we would have such Larks there!* (*Great Expectations* by Charles Dickens)

presently ADV immediately ❑ *I presently knew what they meant* (*Gulliver's Travels* by Jonathan Swift)

pumpion NOUN pumpkin ❑ *for it was almost as large as a small pumpion* (*Gulliver's Travels* by Jonathan Swift)

punctual ADJ kept in one place ❑ *was not a punctual presence, but a spirit* (*The Prelude* by William Wordsworth)

quadrille ◼ NOUN a quadrille is a dance invented in France which is usually performed by four couples ❑ *However, Mr Swiveller had Miss Sophy's hand for the first quadrille (country-dances being low, were utterly proscribed)* (*The Old Curiosity Shop* by Charles Dickens) ◼ NOUN quadrille was a card game for four people ❑ *to make up her pool of quadrille in the evening* (*Pride and Prejudice* by Jane Austen)

quality NOUN gentry or upper-class people ❑ *if you are with the quality*

(*The Adventures of Huckleberry Finn* by Mark Twain)

quick parts phrase quick-witted ❑ *Mr Bennet was so odd a mixture of quick parts* (*Pride and Prejudice* by Jane Austen)

quid NOUN a quid is something chewed or kept in the mouth, like a piece of tobacco ❑ *rolling his quid* (*Treasure Island* by Robert Louis Stevenson)

quit VERB quit means to avenge or to make even ❑ *But Faustus's death shall quit my infamy* (*Doctor Faustus 4.3* by Christopher Marlowe)

rags NOUN divisions ❑ *Nor hours, days, months, which are the rags of time* (*The Sun Rising* by John Donne)

raiment NOUN raiment means clothing ❑ *the mountain shook off turf and flower, had only heath for raiment and crag for gem* (*Jane Eyre* by Charlotte Brontë)

rain cats and dogs phrase an expression meaning rain heavily. The origin of the expression is unclear ❑ *But it'll perhaps rain cats and dogs to-morrow* (*Silas Marner* by George Eliot)

raised Cain phrase raised Cain means caused a lot of trouble. Cain is a character in the Bible who killed his brother Abel ❑ *and every time he got drunk he raised Cain around town* (*The Adventures of Huckleberry Finn* by Mark Twain)

rambling ADJ rambling means confused and not very clear ❑ *my head began to be filled very early with rambling thoughts* (*Robinson Crusoe* by Daniel Defoe)

raree-show NOUN a raree-show is an old term for a peep-show or a fairground entertainment ❑ *A raree-show is here, with children gathered round* (*The Prelude* by William Wordsworth)

recusants NOUN people who resisted authority ❑ *hardy recusants* (*The Prelude* by William Wordsworth)

redounding VERB eddying. An eddy is a movement in water or air which goes round and round instead of flowing in one direction ❑ *mists and steam-like fogs redounding everywhere* (*The Prelude* by William Wordsworth)

redundant ADJ here redundant means overflowing but Wordsworth also uses it to mean excessively large or too big ❑ *A tempest, a redundant energy* (*The Prelude* by William Wordsworth)

reflex NOUN reflex is a shortened version of reflexion, which is an alternative spelling of reflection ❑ *To cut across the reflex of a star* (*The Prelude* by William Wordsworth)

Reformatory NOUN a prison for young offenders/criminals ❑ *Even when I was taken to have a new suit of clothes, the tailor had orders to make them like a kind of Reformatory, and on no account to let me have the free use of my limbs.* (*Great Expectations* by Charles Dickens)

remorse NOUN pity or compassion ❑ *by that remorse* (*On His Mistress* by John Donne)

render VERB in this context render means give. ❑ *and Sarah could render no reason that would be sanctioned by the feeling of the community.* (*Silas Marner* by George Eliot)

repeater NOUN a repeater was a watch that chimed the last hour when a button was pressed – as a result it was useful in the dark ❑ *And his watch is a gold repeater, and worth a hundred pound if it's worth a penny.* (*Great Expectations* by Charles Dickens)

repugnance NOUN repugnance means a strong dislike of something or someone ❑ *overcoming a strong repugnance* (*Treasure Island* by Robert Louis Stevenson)

reverence NOUN reverence means bow. When you bow to someone, you briefly bend your body towards them as a formal way of showing them respect ❑ *made my reverence* (*Gulliver's Travels* by Jonathan Swift)

reverie NOUN a reverie is a day dream ❑ *I can guess the subject of your reverie* (*Pride and Prejudice* by Jane Austen)

revival NOUN a religious meeting held in public ❑ *well I'd ben a-running' a little temperance revival thar' bout a week* (*The Adventures of Huckleberry Finn* by Mark Twain)

revolt VERB revolt means turn back or stop your present course of action and go back to what you were doing before ❑ *Revolt, or I'll in piecemeal tear thy flesh* (*Doctor Faustus 5.1* by Christopher Marlowe)

rheumatics/rheumatism NOUN rheumatics [rheumatism] is an illness that makes your joints or muscles stiff and painful ❑ *a new cure for the rheumatics* (*Treasure Island* by Robert Louis Stevenson)

riddance NOUN riddance is usually used in the form good riddance which you say when you are pleased that something has gone or been left behind ❑ *I'd better go into the house, and die and be a riddance* (*David Copperfield* by Charles Dickens)

rimy ADJ rimy is an ADJECTIVE which means covered in ice or frost ❑ *It was a rimy morning, and very damp* (*Great Expectations* by Charles Dickens)

riper ADJ riper means more mature or older ❑ *At riper years to Wittenberg he went* (*Doctor Faustus chorus* by Christopher Marlowe)

rubber NOUN a set of games in whist or backgammon ❑ *her father was sure of his rubber* (*Emma* by Jane Austen)

ruffian NOUN a ruffian is a person who behaves violently ❑ *and when the ruffian had told him* (*Treasure Island* by Robert Louis Stevenson)

sadness NOUN sadness is an old term meaning seriousness ❑ *But I* prithee tell me, in good sadness (*Doctor Faustus 2.2* by Christopher Marlowe)

sailed before the mast phrase this phrase meant someone who did not look like a sailor ❑ *he had none of the appearance of a man that sailed before the mast* (*Treasure Island* by Robert Louis Stevenson)

scabbard NOUN a scabbard is the covering for a sword or dagger ❑ *Girded round its middle was an antique scabbard; but no sword was in it, and the ancient sheath was eaten up with rust* (*A Christmas Carol* by Charles Dickens)

schooners NOUN A schooner is a fast, medium-sized sailing ship ❑ *if schooners, islands, and maroons* (*Treasure Island* by Robert Louis Stevenson)

science NOUN learning or knowledge ❑ *Even Science, too, at hand* (*The Prelude* by William Wordsworth)

scrouge VERB to scrouge means to squeeze or to crowd ❑ *to scrouge in and get a sight* (*The Adventures of Huckleberry Finn* by Mark Twain)

scrutore NOUN a scrutore, or escritoire, was a writing table ❑ *set me gently on my feet upon the scrutore* (*Gulliver's Travels* by Jonathan Swift)

scutcheon/ escutcheon NOUN an escutcheon is a shield with a coat of arms, or the symbols of a family name, engraved on it ❑ *On the scutcheon we'll have a bend* (*The Adventures of Huckleberry Finn* by Mark Twain)

sea-dog phrase sea-dog is a slang term for an experienced sailor or pirate ❑ *a 'true sea-dog', and a 'real old salt,'* (*Treasure Island* by Robert Louis Stevenson)

see the lions phrase to see the lions was to go and see the sights of London. Originally the phrase referred to the menagerie in the Tower of London and later in Regent's Park ❑ *We will go and see the lions for an hour*

or two – it's something to have a fresh fellow like you to show them to, Copperfield (*David Copperfield* by Charles Dickens)

self-conceit NOUN self-conceit is an old term which means having too high an opinion of oneself, or deceiving yourself ❑ *Till swollen with cunning, of a self-conceit* (*Doctor Faustus chorus* by Christopher Marlowe)

seneschal NOUN a steward ❑ *where a grey-headed seneschal sings a funny chorus with a funnier body of vassals* (*Oliver Twist* by Charles Dickens)

sensible ADJ if you were sensible of something you are aware or conscious of something ❑ *If my children are silly I must hope to be always sensible of it* (*Pride and Prejudice* by Jane Austen)

sessions NOUN court cases were heard at specific times of the year called sessions ❑ *He lay in prison very ill, during the whole interval between his committal for trial, and the coming round of the Sessions.* (*Great Expectations* by Charles Dickens)

shabby ADJ shabby places look old and in bad condition ❑ *a little bit of a shabby village named Pikesville* (*The Adventures of Huckleberry Finn* by Mark Twain)

shay-cart NOUN a shay-cart was a small cart drawn by one horse ❑ *"I were at the Bargemen t'other night, Pip;" whenever he subsided into affection, he called me Pip, and whenever he relapsed into politeness he called me Sir; "when there come up in his shay-cart Pumblechook."* (Great Expectations by Charles Dickens)

shilling NOUN a shilling is an old unit of currency. There were twenty shillings in every British pound ❑ *"Ten shillings too much," said the gentleman in the white waistcoat.* (*Oliver Twist* by Charles Dickens)

shines NOUN tricks or games ❑ *well, it would make a cow laugh to see the* *shines that old idiot cut (The Adventures of Huckleberry Finn by Mark Twain)*

shirking VERB shirking means not doing what you are meant to be doing, or evading your duties ❑ *some of you shirking lubbers (Treasure Island by Robert Louis Stevenson)*

shiver my timbers phrase shiver my timbers is an expression which was used by sailors and pirates to express surprise ❑ *why, shiver my timbers, if I hadn't forgotten my score! (Treasure Island by Robert Louis Stevenson)*

shoe-roses NOUN shoe-roses were roses made from ribbons which were stuck on to shoes as decoration ❑ *the very shoe-roses for Netherfield were got by proxy (Pride and Prejudice by Jane Austen)*

singular ADJ singular means very great and remarkable or strange ❑ *"Singular dream," he says (The Adventures of Huckleberry Finn by Mark Twain)*

sire NOUN sire is an old word which means lord or master or elder ❑ *She also defied her sire (Little Women by Louisa May Alcott)*

sixpence NOUN a sixpence was half of a shilling ❑ *if she had only a shilling in the world, she would be very likely to give away sixpence of it (Emma by Jane Austen)*

slavey NOUN the word slavey was used when there was only one servant in a house or boarding-house – so she had to perform all the duties of a larger staff ❑ *Two distinct knocks, sir, will produce the slavey at any time (The Old Curiosity Shop by Charles Dickens)*

slender ADJ weak ❑ *In slender accents of sweet verse (The Prelude by William Wordsworth)*

slop-shops NOUN slop-shops were shops where cheap ready-made clothes were sold. They mainly sold clothes to sailors ❑ *Accordingly, I took the jacket off, that I might*

learn to do without it; and carrying it under my arm, began a tour of inspection of the various slop-shops. (David Copperfield by Charles Dickens)

sluggard NOUN a lazy person ❑ *"Stand up and repeat 'Tis the voice of the sluggard,'" said the Gryphon. (Alice's Adventures in Wonderland by Lewis Carroll)*

smallpox NOUN smallpox is a serious infectious disease ❑ *by telling the men we had smallpox aboard (The Adventures of Huckleberry Finn by Mark Twain)*

smalls NOUN smalls are short trousers ❑ *It is difficult for a large-headed, small-eyed youth, of lumbering make and heavy countenance, to look dignified under any circumstances; but it is more especially so, when superadded to these personal attractions are a red nose and yellow smalls (Oliver Twist by Charles Dickens)*

sneeze-box NOUN a box for snuff was called a sneeze-box because sniffing snuff makes the user sneeze ❑ *To think of Jack Dawkins — lummy Jack — the Dodger — the Artful Dodger — going abroad for a common twopenny-halfpenny sneeze-box! (Oliver Twist by Charles Dickens)*

snorted VERB slept ❑ *Or snorted we in the Seven Sleepers' den? (The Good-Morrow by John Donne)*

snuff NOUN snuff is tobacco in powder form which is taken by sniffing ❑ *as he thrust his thumb and forefinger into the proffered snuff-box of the undertaker: which was an ingenious little model of a patent coffin. (Oliver Twist by Charles Dickens)*

soliloquized VERB to soliloquize is when an actor in a play speaks to himself or herself rather than to another actor ❑ *"A new servitude! There is something in that," I soliloquized (mentally, be it understood; I did not talk aloud) (Jane Eyre by Charlotte Brontë)*

sough NOUN a sough is a drain or a ditch ❏ *as you may have noticed the sough that runs from the marshes* (*Wuthering Heights* by Emily Brontë)

spirits NOUN a spirit is the nonphysical part of a person which is believed to remain alive after their death ❏ *that I might raise up spirits when I please* (*Doctor Faustus 1.5* by Christopher Marlowe)

spleen ■ NOUN here spleen means a type of sadness or depression which was thought to only affect the wealthy ❏ *yet here I could plainly discover the true seeds of spleen* (*Gulliver's Travels* by Jonathan Swift) ■ NOUN irritability and low spirits ❏ *Adieu to disappointment and spleen* (*Pride and Prejudice* by Jane Austen)

spondulicks NOUN spondulicks is a slang word which means money ❏ *not for all his spondulicks and as much more on top of it* (*The Adventures of Huckleberry Finn* by Mark Twain)

stalled of VERB to be stalled of something is to be bored with it ❏ *I'm stalled of doing naught* (*Wuthering Heights* by Emily Brontë)

stanchion NOUN a stanchion is a pole or bar that stands upright and is used as a buidling support ❏ *and slid down a stanchion* (*The Adventures of Huckleberry Finn* by Mark Twain)

stang NOUN stang is another word for pole which was an old measurement ❏ *These fields were intermingled with woods of half a stang* (*Gulliver's Travels* by Jonathan Swift)

starlings NOUN a starling is a wall built around the pillars that support a bridge to protect the pillars ❏ *There were states of the tide when, having been down the river, I could not get back through the eddy-chafed arches and starlings of old London Bridge* (*Great Expectations* by Charles Dickens)

startings NOUN twitching or night-time movements of the body ❏ *with midnight's startings* (*On His Mistress* by John Donne)

stomacher NOUN a panel at the front of a dress ❏ *but send her aunt the pattern of a stomacher* (*Emma* by Jane Austen)

stoop VERB swoop ❏ *Once a kite hovering over the garden made a swoop at me* (*Gulliver's Travels* by Jonathan Swift)

succedaneum NOUN a succedaneum is a substitute ❏ *But as a succedaneum* (*The Prelude* by William Wordsworth)

suet NOUN a hard animal fat used in cooking ❏ *and your jaws are too weak For anything tougher than suet* (*Alice's Adventures in Wonderland* by Lewis Carroll)

sultry ADJ sultry weather is hot and damp. Here sultry means unpleasant or risky ❏ *for it was getting pretty sultry for us* (*The Adventures of Huckleberry Finn* by Mark Twain)

summerset NOUN summerset is an old spelling of somersault. If someone does a somersault, they turn over completely in the air ❏ *I have seen him do the summerset* (*Gulliver's Travels* by Jonathan Swift)

supper NOUN supper was a light meal taken late in the evening. The main meal was dinner which was eaten at four or five in the afternoon ❏ *and the supper table was all set out* (*Emma* by Jane Austen)

surfeits VERB to surfeit in something is to have far too much of it, or to overindulge in it to an unhealthy degree ❏ *He surfeits upon cursed necromancy* (*Doctor Faustus chorus* by Christopher Marlowe)

surtout NOUN a surtout is a long close-fitting overcoat ❏ *He wore a long black surtout reaching nearly to his ankles* (*The Old Curiosity Shop* by Charles Dickens)

swath NOUN swath is the width of corn cut by a scythe ❏ *while thy* *hook Spares the next swath* (*Ode to Autumn* by John Keats)

sylvan ADJ sylvan means belonging to the woods ❏ *Sylvan historian* (*Ode on a Grecian Urn* by John Keats)

taction NOUN taction means touch. This means that the people had to be touched on the mouth or the ears to get their attention ❏ *without being roused by some external taction upon the organs of speech and hearing* (*Gulliver's Travels* by Jonathan Swift)

Tag and Rag and Bobtail phrase the riff-raff, or lower classes. Used in an insulting way ❏ *"No," said he; "not till it got about that there was no protection on the premises, and it come to be considered dangerous, with convicts and Tag and Rag and Bobtail going up and down."* (*Great Expectations* by Charles Dickens)

tallow NOUN tallow is hard animal fat that is used to make candles and soap ❏ *and a lot of tallow candles* (*The Adventures of Huckleberry Finn* by Mark Twain)

tan VERB to tan means to beat or whip ❏ *and if I catch you about that school I'll tan you good* (*The Adventures of Huckleberry Finn* by Mark Twain)

tanyard NOUN the tanyard is part of a tannery, which is a place where leather is made from animal skins ❏ *hid in the old tanyard* (*The Adventures of Huckleberry Finn* by Mark Twain)

tarry ADJ tarry means the colour of tar or black ❏ *his tarry pig-tail* (*Treasure Island* by Robert Louis Stevenson)

thereof phrase from there ❏ *By all desires which thereof did ensue* (*On His Mistress* by John Donne)

thick with, be phrase if you are 'thick with someone' you are very close, sharing secrets – it is often used to describe people who are planning something secret ❏ *Hasn't he been thick with Mr*

Heathcliff lately? (*Wuthering Heights* by Emily Brontë)

thimble NOUN a thimble is a small cover used to protect the finger while sewing ❏ *The paper had been sealed in several places by a thimble* (*Treasure Island* by Robert Louis Stevenson)

thirtover ADJ thirtover is an old word which means obstinate or that someone is very determined to do want they want and can not be persuaded to do something in another way ❏ *I have been living on in a thirtover, lackadaisical way* (*Tess of the D'Urbervilles* by Thomas Hardy)

timbrel NOUN timbrel is a tambourine ❏ *What pipes and timbrels?* (*Ode on a Grecian Urn* by John Keats)

tin NOUN tin is slang for money/cash ❏ *Then the plain question is, an't it a pity that this state of things should continue, and how much better would it be for the old gentleman to hand over a reasonable amount of tin, and make it all right and comfortable* (*The Old Curiosity Shop* by Charles Dickens)

tincture NOUN a tincture is a medicine made with alcohol and a small amount of a drug ❏ *with ink composed of a cephalic tincture* (*Gulliver's Travels* by Jonathan Swift)

tithe NOUN a tithe is a tax paid to the church ❏ *and held farms which, speaking from a spiritual point of view, paid highly-desirable tithes* (*Silas Marner* by George Eliot)

towardly ADJ a towardly child is dutiful or obedient ❏ *and a towardly child* (*Gulliver's Travels* by Jonathan Swift)

toys NOUN trifles are things which are considered to have little importance, value, or significance ❏ *purchase my life from them bysome bracelets, glass rings, and other toys* (*Gulliver's Travels* by Jonathan Swift)

tract NOUN a tract is a religious pamphlet or leaflet ❏ *and Joe*

Harper got a hymn-book and a tract (*The Adventures of Huckleberry Finn* by Mark Twain)

train-oil NOUN train-oil is oil from whale blubber ❏ *The train-oil and gunpowder were shoved out of sight in a minute* (*Wuthering Heights* by Emily Brontë)

tribulation NOUN tribulation means the suffering or difficulty you experience in a particular situation ❏ *Amy was learning this distinction through much tribulation* (*Little Women* by Louisa May Alcott)

trivet NOUN a trivet is a three-legged stand for resting a pot or kettle ❏ *a pocket-knife in his right; and a pewter pot on the trivet* (*Oliver Twist* by Charles Dickens)

trot line NOUN a trot line is a fishing line to which a row of smaller fishing lines are attached ❏ *when he got along I was hard at it taking up a trot line* (*The Adventures of Huckleberry Finn* by Mark Twain)

troth NOUN oath or pledge ❏ *I wonder, by my troth* (*The Good-Morrow* by John Donne)

truckle NOUN a truckle bedstead is a bed that is on wheels and can be slid under another bed to save space ❏ *It rose under my hand, and the door yielded. Looking in, I saw a lighted candle on a table, a bench, and a mattress on a truckle bedstead.* (*Great Expectations* by Charles Dickens)

trump NOUN a trump is a good, reliable person wo can be trusted ❏ *This lad Hawkins is a trump, I perceive* (*Treasure Island* by Robert Louis Stevenson)

tucker NOUN a tucker is a frilly lace collar which is worn around the neck ❏ *Whereat Scrooge's niece's sister˜the plump one with the lace tucker: not the one with the roses˜blushed.* (*A Christmas Carol* by Charles Dickens)

tureen NOUN a large bowl with a lid from which soup or vegetables are served ❏ *Waiting in a hot tureen!* (*Alice's Adventures in Wonderland* by Lewis Carroll)

turnkey NOUN a prison officer; jailer ❏ *As we came out of the prison through the lodge, I found that the great importance of my guardian was appreciated by the turnkeys, no less than by those whom they held in charge.* (*Great Expectations* by Charles Dickens)

turnpike NOUN the upkeep of many roads of the time was paid for by tolls (fees) collected at posts along the road. There was a gate to prevent people travelling further along the road until the toll had been paid. ❏ *Traddles, whom I have taken up by appointment at the turnpike, presents a dazzling combination of cream colour and light blue; and both he and Mr. Dick have a general effect about them of being all gloves.* (*David Copperfield* by Charles Dickens)

twas phrase it was ❏ *twas but a dream of thee* (*The Good-Morrow* by John Donne)

tyrannized VERB tyrannized means bullied or forced to do things against their will ❏ *for people would soon cease coming there to be tyrannized over and put down* (*Treasure Island* by Robert Louis Stevenson)

'un NOUN 'un is a slang term for one – usually used to refer to a person ❏ *She's been thinking the old 'un* (*David Copperfield* by Charles Dickens)

undistinguished ADJ undiscriminating or incapable of making a distinction between good and bad things ❏ *their undistinguished appetite to devour everything* (*Gulliver's Travels* by Jonathan Swift)

use NOUN habit ❏ *Though use make you apt to kill me* (*The Flea* by John Donne)

vacant ADJ vacant usually means empty, but here Wordsworth uses it to mean carefree ❏ *To vacant musing, unreproved neglect* (*The Prelude* by William Wordsworth)

valetudinarian NOUN one too concerned with his or her own health. ❏ *for having been a valetudinarian all his life* (*Emma* by Jane Austen)

vamp VERB vamp means to walk or tramp to somewhere ❏ *Well, vamp on to Marlott, will 'ee* (*Tess of the D'Urbervilles* by Thomas Hardy)

vapours NOUN the vapours is an old term which means unpleasant and strange thoughts, which make the person feel nervous and unhappy ❏ *and my head was full of vapours* (*Robinson Crusoe* by Daniel Defoe)

vegetables NOUN here vegetables means plants ❏ *the other vegetables are in the same proportion* (*Gulliver's Travels* by Jonathan Swift)

venturesome ADJ if you are venturesome you are willing to take risks ❏ *he must be either hopelessly stupid or a venturesome fool* (*Wuthering Heights* by Emily Brontë)

verily ADJ verily means really or truly ❏ *though I believe verily* (*Robinson Crusoe* by Daniel Defoe)

vicinage NOUN vicinage is an area or the residents of an area ❏ *and to his thought the whole vicinage was haunted by her.* (*Silas Marner* by George Eliot)

victuals NOUN victuals means food ❏ *grumble a little over the victuals* (*The Adventures of Huckleberry Finn* by Mark Twain)

vintage NOUN vintage in this context means wine ❏ *Oh, for a draught of vintage!* (*Ode on a Nightingale* by John Keats)

virtual ADJ here virtual means powerful or strong ❏ *had virtual faith* (*The Prelude* by William Wordsworth)

vittles NOUN vittles is a slang word which means food ❏ *There never was such a woman for givin' away vittles and drink* (*Little Women* by Louisa May Alcott)

voided straight phrase voided straight is an old expression which means emptied immediately ❏ *see the rooms be voided straight* (*Doctor Faustus 4.1* by Christopher Marlowe)

wainscot NOUN wainscot is wood panel lining in a room so wainscoted means a room lined with wooden panels ❏ *in the dark wainscoted parlor* (*Silas Marner* by George Eliot)

walking the plank phrase walking the plank was a punishment in which a prisoner would be made to walk along a plank on the side of the ship and fall into the sea, where they would be abandoned ❏ *about hanging, and walking the plank* (*Treasure Island* by Robert Louis Stevenson)

want VERB want means to be lacking or short of ❏ *The next thing wanted was to get the picture framed* (*Emma* by Jane Austen)

wanting ADJ wanting means lacking or missing ❏ *wanting two fingers of the left hand* (*Treasure Island* by Robert Louis Stevenson)

wanting, I was not phrase I was not wanting means I did not fail ❏ *I was not wanting to lay a foundation of religious knowledge in his mind* (*Robinson Crusoe* by Daniel Defoe)

ward NOUN a ward is, usually, a child who has been put under the protection of the court or a guardian for his or her protection ❏ *I call the Wards in Jarndyce. The are caged up with all the others.* (*Bleak House* by Charles Dickens)

waylay VERB to waylay someone is to lie in wait for them or to intercept them ❏ *I must go up the road and waylay him* (*The Adventures of Huckleberry Finn* by Mark Twain)

weazen NOUN weazen is a slang word for throat. It actually means shrivelled ❏ *You with an uncle too! Why, I knowed you at Gargery's when you was so small a wolf that I could have took your weazen betwixt this finger and thumb and chucked* *you away dead* (*Great Expectations* by Charles Dickens)

wery ◧ ADV very ❑ *Be wery careful o' vidders all your life* (*Pickwick Papers* by Charles Dickens) ◪ See wibrated

wherry NOUN wherry is a small swift rowing boat for one person ❑ *It was flood tide when Daniel Quilp sat himself down in the wherry to cross to the opposite shore.* (*The Old Curiosity Shop* by Charles Dickens)

whether prep whether means which of the two in this example ❑ *we came in full view of a great island or continent (for we knew not whether)* (*Gulliver's Travels* by Jonathan Swift)

whetstone NOUN a whetstone is a stone used to sharpen knives and other tools ❑ *I dropped pap's whetstone there too* (*The Adventures of Huckleberry Finn* by Mark Twain)

wibrated VERB in Dickens's use of the English language 'w' often replaces 'v' when he is reporting speech. So here 'wibrated' means 'vibrated'. In Pickwick Papers a judge asks Sam Weller (who constantly confuses the two letters) 'Do you spell is with a 'v' or a 'w'?' to which Weller replies 'That depends upon the taste and fancy of the speller, my Lord' ❑ *There are strings . . . in the human heart that had better not be wibrated'* (*Barnaby Rudge* by Charles Dickens)

wicket NOUN a wicket is a little door in a larger entrance ❑ *Having rested here, for a minute or so, to collect a good burst of sobs and an imposing show of tears and terror, he knocked loudly at the wicket;* (*Oliver Twist* by Charles Dickens)

without CONJ without means unless ❑ *You don't know about me, without you have read a book by the name of The Adventures of Tom Sawyer* (*The Adventures of Huckleberry Finn* by Mark Twain)

wittles ◧ NOUN vittles is a slang word which means food ❑ *I live on broken wittles – and I sleep on the coals* (*David Copperfield* by Charles Dickens) ◪ See wibrated

woo VERB courts or forms a proper relationship with ❑ *before it woo* (*The Flea* by John Donne)

words, to have phrase if you have words with someone you have a disagreement or an argument ❑ *I do not want to have words with a young thing like you.* (*Black Beauty* by Emily Brontë)

workhouse NOUN workhouses were places where the homeless were given food and a place to live in return for doing very hard work ❑ *And the Union workhouses? demanded Scrooge. Are they still in operation?* (A Christmas Carol by Charles Dickens)

yawl NOUN a yawl is a small boat kept on a bigger boat for short trips. Yawl is also the name for a small fishing boat ❑ *She sent out her yawl, and we went aboard* (*The Adventures of Huckleberry Finn* by Mark Twain)

yeomanry NOUN the yeomanry was a collective term for the middle classes involved in agriculture ❑ *The yeomanry are precisely the order of people with whom I feel I can have nothing to do* (*Emma* by Jane Austen)

yonder ADV yonder means over there ❑ *all in the same second we seem to hear low voices in yonder!* (*The Adventures of Huckleberry Finn* by Mark Twain)